MW01119823

all things

a Rev. Alma Lee Mystery
(book 1)

by Amber Belldene

Copyright © 2018 Amber Belldene

All rights reserved.

ISBN-13: 978-0-9972211-6-9

.

All things bright and beautiful,
All creatures great and small,
All things wise and wonderful:
The Lord God made them all.

- an English hymn by Cecil F. Alexander, 1848

Chapter One

It started at The Carlos Club, San Francisco's one and only lesbian bar. That's me over there in the corner—the Reverend Alma Lee, vicar, agitator, despiser of 90's dance music—slamming my hip into the jukebox with all my weight behind it.

"Everybody Dance Now" died its last thump of bass. *Thank you, Jesus*. Cheers and applause broke out in the crowded bar. I raised my hand to acknowledge the approval, then dropped two quarters in the slot and selected K-249. The coins clinked inside the machine, and the song began to play. Johnny Cash, "Ring of Fire."

I blew out a breath. Much more fitting for the solemn occasion—the death of a landmark, an icon—the closing party for the city's one and only dyke bar.

I stroked my hand over the flickering orange and red lights of the machine. Cindy had sold it on Craig's List for $400 to someone who'd agreed to pick it up tomorrow—before the landlord arrived to haul away whatever she'd left and sell it himself.

At the end of the long, narrow room, Cindy waved her thick, tattooed arms at me. What now?

For years, I'd coached my friend on how to keep her bar in the black. Craft cocktails, a fresh coat of paint, no more cracked vinyl booths—she had to cater to the gentrifying neighborhood. But Cindy considered changing anything about the dive selling out. Which meant when the landlord hiked up her rent, the price of her authenticity was eviction.

"Alma, hey! Looking good." Chelle, a regular at the dive, pushed between two clusters of women to reach me. She had the

1

build of one of Wonder Woman's Amazon sisters. From my barely five feet, I had to look up miles to see her face. Along the way, I admired her tight white tank top, which showed off her flawless dark skin and featured a sequined rainbow with a unicorn beneath it.

"Nice shirt."

"Thanks." She bent to kiss my cheek. "Great party."

"What can I say?" I raised my voice to be heard over Johnny Cash and a hundred women drowning their sorrows in $2 well drinks. "I know how to throw a wake."

Chelle chuckled hoarsely. "I guess you would, the high priestess of Mission Street."

I'd landed the nickname when I helped organize a rally to defend a medical marijuana dispensary from losing its lease to a national bank branch. We'd won that battle, and I kind of liked the alias… As long as my bishop didn't hear of it.

Someone drew Chelle away. Behind her, leaning against the bar, a brunette beauty I'd never seen bobbed her head to "Ring of Fire" and drank something out of a highball glass through a straw. God, what a mouth—so wide, such red lips.

She wore glasses with a slight horn-rim shape. From behind the lenses, she spotted me and held my stare.

I raised my chin. She drew the straw from between her lips and smiled at me.

Score.

I bee lined for her.

Cindy leapt out, her matronly bosom heaving in her purple tank top, damp with sweat. "Thank God, there you are."

Damn.

I clenched my teeth. "Here I am."

"We've got a big problem."

I glanced over at Ms. Drinks-cocktails-with-straws. A chick with a salt-and-pepper buzz cut was chatting her up.

I contained my sigh.

Cindy and I'd been friends since high school, closer some years than others. After her landlord had taped an eviction notice to the door ninety days ago, she'd barely been able to pee without me holding her hand, which was frankly closer than I preferred. We'd organized rallies, press conferences, and fundraisers, but none of it was enough to keep her lease because she had the business sense of the houseplant drooping in her office.

"What happened?"

She combed her fingers through her purple bob, sweaty at the roots. "Somebody called the cops, and we're way over the occupancy limit."

I glanced at the door. Two officers in blue stood just inside.

"Right." With one last winsome glance at my brunette, I veered in the opposite direction. Cindy only needed my help one more night.

Six feet away, I saw one of the cops was Mario and faltered as if an invisible rubber band was pulling me back toward the sexy stranger. I took a deep breath and pushed through the resistance.

"Hey, Mario."

At twenty-seven, the kid still had a round-cheeked baby face. He smiled, his brown eyes creasing. "Alma. Long time."

Thirteen months and eleven days since the night his big brother Cesar had dumped me at their mama's fiftieth birthday party. But who was counting?

"Hey, good to see you." I shook his hand. "What are you doing here?"

Mario's trim, blond partner scanned the crowd, blue eyes bright with curiosity. But Mario surveyed me, probably looking for details to report to his brother. "Dispatch said somebody upstairs complained about the noise."

I glanced at the ceiling. I'd personally invited the tenants of both the Victorian's flats, and I'd seen them all at the party.

"As a matter of fact, everyone who lives upstairs is here. I'm guessing the landlord phoned in a complaint just to be a pill. This is the closing party, and he's been harassing Cindy for months. The noise isn't bothering him. He lives across town. We're not even being that loud."

The *Maximum Occupancy 88* sign hung on the wall right behind Mario's head. *Please don't look.*

Mario scanned the room over my shoulder, the doughy features of his face not as stern as he meant them to be. His partner watched me through narrowed eyes, trying to figure out why Mario was giving me an inch.

Finally, he shrugged. "All right. But keep it quiet, okay? And wrap things up on time."

I grinned. "You got it. I owe you one."

3

"Nah." He waved his hand in the air, turning and calling over his shoulder. "We look out for each other."

Blondie tipped her head toward him as they walked out. I could practically hear him telling her, *That's my brother's lesbian ex-girlfriend.*

The woman scratched her scalp beneath her tight ponytail.

Yeah, honey. Cesar and me make me scratch my head too, but that's all over now.

I spun to look for my brunette. There she was, still at the bar, talking to a guy with a mop of thick curls.

Please, Jesus, let him be her friend.

As if she could feel me stare, she looked straight at me, then away with a coy smile.

My heart pitter-pattered a quick beat. This would be fun.

A microphone crackled. Cindy had climbed up to stand on the bar. She hadn't bothered to dress for a special occasion, but wore her usual ratty jeans and Chucks, her prematurely gray hair died the same lavender as her tank top. "I want to thank everyone for coming tonight. It's been a hell of a ride all these years."

People straightened and turned, whooping and cheering. Even as a half-pint, it was tricky to move between them unobtrusively when they stood still and facing her. I stopped next to the jukebox—I didn't want her to notice me skulking my way to the brunette instead of listening, like that one distracting person glued to his phone screen during my sermon.

Cindy called out names and thanked people who'd helped our campaign. She glowed, looking more like herself than she had in months. I blew out a breath. It was finally over, and she could move on.

Rubbing her palms together, she swayed atop the bar. How many rum and diet cokes had she drunk?

She waved her arm over the crowd, the way I moved mine over bread and wine on Sunday mornings. "Seeing you all, I've been thinking I gave up too soon."

I froze. *No, no, no.* It wasn't too soon. Not unless she planned to make major changes to her business model, tend bar and clean the bathrooms herself. And she had so much debt—

"Hell, no, we won't go." The chant erupted from behind me.

I covered my eyes with my palm. This was not the farewell speech we'd discussed.

I shook my head, trying to get Cindy's attention.

She noticed and beamed at me. "And now I'd like to call up Alma Lee, who's been busting her ass to save this place. Tell us what we do next, Alma. How do we keep the fight going?"

"Alma!" People called my name, whistled loudly.

Crap. With a tug, Cindy pulled me up onto the bar.

The room grew silent, awaiting my instructions. I looked down at the crowd. How could I get this back under control without saying that the death of The Carlos Club was as much Cindy's fault as it was a greedy landlord's?

Gripping the mic with both hands, I began. "I won't lie. It sucks that we didn't win this one. It sucks that after a long day, I won't be able to take off my collar and skip across the street for a night cap."

"Leave on the collar, baby. It's hot."

"Don't be creepy, Pam. I'm not your fetish." I wagged my finger. A riot of laughter gave me another few seconds to think.

"This city is changing too damn fast. But it's still our city. We won't let anybody take it away from us. We'll gather in the parks and on the street. We'll hang out with our brothers at the Hawk. We'll make new safe places. And you're always welcome at St. Giles'."

"Morning Prayer every day at 8:30 a.m. Sunday services at 9," my parishioner Tish called out. I saluted her.

"Tonight, we say goodbye to The Carlos Club, but that isn't the end of our story. Tomorrow is a new day, and it's whatever we want to make it."

The crowd of slightly drunk women cheered. My preaching professor would have critiqued my pseudo-inspirational vagaries, but the audience at my feet didn't seem to mind.

Cindy blinked at me. She'd figure it out eventually. I gave her arm a quick squeeze and scanned the crowd for my brunette.

Were those her shiny dark waves swishing their way towards the back patio? I vaulted off the bar and gave chase.

The patio housed a few smokers and a pair of idle gas heaters. Cindy couldn't afford to fill the propane tanks.

My girl sat at a picnic table, her face lit up by the screen of her phone. Up close, she was a portrait of beautiful particulars: a thin scar bisected her right eyebrow and made its white way half an inch up her ivory forehead. Her ear was a pretty little spiral shell.

"Hi."

She glanced up and smiled. A narrow gap divided her front teeth, and a fleck of her red lipstick clung to one. "Hi."

My mouth went dry.

"Alma, right?" she asked.

She remembered! Still, I played it cool, like I wasn't doing an internal victory dance. "Yeah, that's right."

"Nice speech."

I raised a shoulder. "It was kind of lame."

"Sometimes lame is all they need."

"True." One of my buddies from seminary might offer the same advice, which begged a question. "Do you do a lot of public speaking?"

"You could say that."

Okay. So pillow lips was a bit cryptic. It suited her coy half-smile.

She fingered a pendent on a silver chain. "I'm Naomi." She dropped her pendant down the front of her blouse and extended her long, fair arm. Somehow, the gesture put distance between us, even as I slid my hot palm against her long, cool fingertips.

"Alma."

She squeezed back. "Yeah, I know."

Wow, Alma, where is your game tonight? I grinned, refusing to flinch or otherwise show she'd flustered me.

"How come I haven't seen you here before?"

"I'm new in town. Moved from the East Coast for a job last month, which might just make me one of the loathsome yuppies everybody in there is badmouthing."

I hoisted myself up on the picnic table, sitting above her seat on the bench at a right angle that hopefully downplayed my interest.

"Believe me, there's more to the story of the decline of The Carlos Club than merely gentrification."

"There's a million versions of every story, aren't there?" She stood, putting herself at my eye level.

Was she going to leave already? *Quick, ask a question to keep her here.*

"Do you work in tech?" Most of the yuppies did.

"Nope." Again, she fiddled with her pendant. "But I like this game." She caught her lower lip under the tooth with the lipstick on it and narrowed her eyes. "You work at a church across the street, and you wear a collar. Giles isn't a likely name for a Lutheran parish or some other protestant denomination. So that makes you... an Episcopal priest?"

I pulled my gaze off that kissable mouth to see her brown eyes up close behind her glasses. "Wow, I'm impressed, Sherlock."

She winked. "Elementary, my dear Alma."

A funny feeling stirred in my belly, one I hadn't felt in at least thirteen months and eleven days. "Maybe I could show you around town, help you get to know your new home?"

"Maybe you could." She tucked a lock of hair behind her ear.

"What do you like to do in your free time?"

"The usual stuff." She ran her hand through her hair, dislodging the lock she'd just tucked.

She wore a thick silver bracelet engraved with words. I lifted her hand, gently twisting her wrist so I could read the text. *See! The winter is past; the rains are over and gone.*

"That's from the *Song of Songs*."

"Is it?" The pitch of her voice rose with sarcasm.

I held up my palms. "No need to prickle. People quote the Bible all the time, thinking it's Shakespeare or Martin Luther King."

She laughed from her belly as she withdrew her hand. "True."

"Did you move here to put the winter behind you?"

She met my gaze, her irises flickering with deliberation. "That's a long story. I'll tell you another time."

"Promise?"

"I don't make promises to strangers."

"We aren't strangers. You know everything about me."

"Hardly." She laughed again. Hopefully she liked funny girls.

"So tell me something about you." I reached for her waist, and she let me draw her closer.

"Hm. Well, my favorite flavor of ice cream is salted caramel."

"Mine too! Clearly we have a lot in common." For obvious reasons, I left out the part about how I only ate soy or coconut frozen desserts. I'd learned it was wiser to save the I'm-a-vegan reveal for second dates.

She poked my sternum. "I bet you say that to all the girls."

"Nope. Just you."

"Really?" She quirked a brow up over the frame of her glasses.

I pulled her closer. "Can I kiss you?"

A faint blush bloomed on Naomi's cheekbones. "Okay. But just once."

With her lips millimeters from mine, shouting reached me from inside the bar. I ignored it.

She stiffened under my hands and pulled away. "That's my brother's voice."

Reluctantly, I recognized the second shouter—Cindy. Irritation and duty warred in me. Responsibility won. "It sounds like they're in the office. It's this way."

I hadn't needed to say it. She already had her hand on the door, just inside the back hallway, rank with the smell of stale beer and urine. I reached her as she swung it open, revealing the man with a pile of curls who'd been with her at the bar. He stood nose to nose with Cindy, as close as I'd been to Naomi seconds earlier. Only, their fists were curled and their voices raised.

"If you don't close down tonight, I'll have the cops here first thing tomorrow."

"Just you try. Alma knows them all—they're on our side." She waved at me as if she'd known I'd appear precisely at the crucial moment in her argument.

I stepped forward. "Well, I wouldn't say they're on—"

"I put everything into my plans for this place." Red-faced, the man spun away from Cindy, flinging his fists down, his arms rigid at his sides.

Naomi got hold of his wrist. "David, calm down. This isn't the way to solve problems."

His voice cracked. "If my lease on this place falls through, I'll lose everything."

"I know it feels that way." She squeezed his shoulder. "But you'll find another space."

He shook his head, deflated, the color draining from his face. "You don't understand. This is everything…"

Cindy rolled her eyes. "Will you two get the hell out of my office? I need to talk to Alma about our plans."

Naomi tugged her brother toward the door. I stepped aside at the threshold to let them through. She met my gaze and pulled a tight smile.

"Can I call you?" I whispered.

She jerked her head to the side. "Not a good idea. It was nice to meet you, though."

With a hand on the doorframe, I watched her lead her brother down the smelly hallway.

A thud behind me made me turn. Cindy had dropped into her derelict desk chair, which somehow remained upright at a slant of at least nine degrees.

She glowered at me. "Sleeping with the enemy?"

If only…

She rummaged on her untidy desk. "So, tell me if you think this will work. We go out there and ask the girls to show up bright and early tomorrow…" She found a semi-blank cocktail napkin and an ink pen, holding them up triumphantly.

Right there, we already had a flaw in her plan. Ask a bar full of drunken women to come back first thing in the morning? This was Cindy's problem, not an ounce of pragmatism in that purple head of hers.

"Cin—"

She drew stick figures on the napkin, which already featured a frowny face and read *J/K!*—the abbreviation for just kidding. It was easy to imagine Cindy passing the note as an apology to someone she'd offended with one of her too honest jokes. She held up her diagram. "And we'll make a human chain like this around the buil—"

"Cin—"

"When the landlord's demo team shows up—"

"No!"

She blinked at me. "The human chain's a bad idea?"

"The whole thing is a bad idea. We lost this fight for a reason. It's time to regroup, figure out what's next for you, and move on."

Her jaw fell open, and her pleasant features twisted into fury. "Are you trying to cozy up to that girl?"

Anger boiled through me. I inhaled and blew it out on the next breath. Thou Shalt Not Murder, and all that.

"Yes, I was trying to cozy up to her, but that's not why it's time for you to throw in the towel." I fingered a waxy, sallow leaf on her *Philodendron.* "Cindy—you're a lousy business woman. You were a better social worker. Hell, you were a better barista."

Her lower lip trembled.

"I'm sorry to have to say it like that, but it's true."

She pointed at the door. "Get out."

"Don't be—"

"Get out."

9

And so I did. We could discuss it tomorrow, when she was sober, and no longer the proprietor of The Carlos Club.

Chapter Two

The next morning, I bounded out of bed, ready to face my day.

The postage-stamp sized house where I lived behind St. Giles' had originally been built as a shelter after the 1906 earthquake. Once there'd been a whole row of them on a deep, narrow lot that faced Fifteenth Street and ran through the center of the block. Decades back, a developer bought the property from the city to tear them down and build apartments. A history buff on the vestry of St. Giles' put up his own money to save the one nearest to the church for posterity, and to house their beloved bachelor rector at the time.

The house didn't have enough windows and was overdue for a kitchen and bathroom remodel, but I loved my little vicarage. Plus, I'd never have made it to 8:30 a.m. Morning Prayer five days a week if I lived half a block further from St. Giles'.

Even with such proximity, I was known to stumble in at 8:35, and the altar guild no longer begrudged me my mug of gunpowder green tea. Uncaffeinated, I can scare the pants off any fierce old lady, no matter how much she wants to protect the needlepoint pew cushions from spills.

Freshly showered, my hair still wet, I walked down the path alongside the sanctuary. I rounded the building and ascended the stairs, searching my ring for the big skeleton key to the narthex one handed, while my mug steamed in the other. Before I reached the top step, something appeared in my field of vision. A person in a black coat curled into the fetal position.

Sometimes transients slept under the overhang. I knew most of them by name and had an individualized strategy for waking each one without inciting profanity or violence. Alice responded best to firm pats on her shoulder. Phil roused most peacefully when I quietly sang "Rise and Shine." Still, best to keep back several steps from him just in case he shot to his feet, frightened and ready to throw a punch.

At first glance, I didn't recognize this person. I bent closer and caught sight of purple hair peeking out of a black hood. I knew that dye job, but not from my stoop sleepers.

"Cindy?"

She didn't move. The color of her skin was wrong—not her usually ruddy cheeks, but pallid, almost gray. Then I saw the blood matted in her hair and trailing down her face. I dropped my mug of tea.

I had no doubt she was dead.

Cindy, who I'd met in Algebra II class in tenth grade. Who got me stoned the one and only time I'd ever smoked pot. Who kindly got me drunk at her bar many times in the months after Cesar dumped me, whose hand I had held for the last ninety days. Cindy, whom I'd parted with angrily.

She was dead.

I dropped to my knees and did what every priest worth the price of her vestments would do when words failed. I recited a prayer, straight from the book.

"Into your hands, O Lord, I commend your servant Cindy. Acknowledge a sheep of your own fold, a lamb of your own flock. Receive her into the arms of your mercy, into the blessed rest of everlasting peace, and into the glorious company of the saints in light. Amen."

I brushed the hair off her forehead. The blood made it stick to my fingers. Right. Probably shouldn't be touching her.

I pulled out my phone. My arm felt a mile long. I dialed the Mission Street police dispatch. I had the number on speed dial for the many nuisances that came with leading a church in the eclectic neighborhood, including when Alice or Phil did not take kindly to being roused from sleep.

Cindy would never wake up.

"I'd like to report a dead body." I heard my voice echo in my ears as if I was outside my skin.

The sirens sounded moments later, leaving the station four blocks away.

I answered the dispatcher's questions—Was I hurt? Was there anyone nearby? All I could think was *Cindy. Cindy. Cindy.* Today was supposed to be her new start. And someone would have to tell Lynn her wife was dead.

The black-and-white cars pulled up. Two cops I'd never met gently tugged me away from the body.

The female officer handed me a tissue. I touched my cheek and found it damp with tears.

"Is there someplace we can talk?" asked the male officer.

"I don't want to leave her. She's my friend." And I'd been a lousy one to her last night, storming off in anger. If I'd stayed at the party, helped her close up one last time, would she still be alive?

The squeal of tires jerked me out of my regret-filled thoughts. A dark Ford SUV U-turned in the middle of the block, cutting off a line of cars in the opposite lane. The unmarked truck parked halfway on the red-curbed sidewalk, facing the oncoming traffic.

Cesar burst out of the driver's door in one of his black suits, too well cut to mark him as a homicide detective.

Relief settled on me, slowed my thoughts, as if some unconscious part of me believed he made everything okay. I hated him for that.

"Alls?"

My nickname since the fifth grade. Only he still used it.

I flung my arm toward where she lay. "It's Cindy."

"Damn." He breathed the word, glancing over his shoulder at the bar. "Mario said he saw you there last night."

"Hey boss," a third uniformed officer said, "looks like a blow to the head. You can see a trail of blood that leads across the street from the bar. She has her phone on her, with credit cards and cash stuffed in its wallet case."

"Block off the street. Get the blood trail photographed pronto."

"Yes, sir." The young man loped off, speaking into the radio.

Cesar came to my side.

"I left her." My breaths were coming fast, too fast. "I shouldn't have left her. She needed me."

He punched my shoulder, hard. "No. You don't get to do that. Alma Lee does not get hysterical. Unless you hit her over the head yourself, snap out of it and be useful."

He was right. I hated him for that, too.

13

"I smell smoke." The officer who'd given me a tissue scanned Cindy as if looking for a bullet wound.

"It's my tea. I dropped it when I saw her." I pointed at my mug, shattered at the bottom of the stairs.

Cesar snorted.

"So much for securing the crime scene," the officer muttered.

Cesar took hold of my elbow and led me around the corner of the church to the office. I handed him my massive key ring. "Yellow one."

He unlocked the door. Soon, my parish administrator would arrive, but at the moment the tidy reception area where she worked was dark. I didn't need Cesar's inevitable commentary about my messy office, so I flipped on the lights in the front room and cranked up the thermostat.

I needed caffeine, and I'd spilled my tea on Cindy… No. Not her. Her corpse…

The swirling knot of emotions tried to rise up my throat again. I swallowed them to avoid getting punched out of my hysterics a second time. After flipping on the kettle, I spooned tea pellets into a new mug, emblazoned with my seminary seal. I pictured the one shattered on the sidewalk and sniffled. It had read *HBIC*, short for Head Bitch In Charge, a gift from my pal Jordan. Although whenever a parishioner asked, I said it was from a conference I'd attended.

"Talk to me." Cesar perched his big, muscular frame on my neat-freak parish administrator's immaculate desk. "What got Cindy killed?"

"You know her." I jabbed his chest. He couldn't investigate the death of someone he knew personally, which meant he was just trying to get me talking so I didn't crumble again before the official detective assigned to the case arrived.

"Yeah, and in theory the chief would assign somebody else. But we've got three guys out on leave, and two working that shooting at the liquor store. Chances are, he won't take me off, now that I'm here. So spill. Who'd want Cindy dead?"

"God, I don't know. Don't people only want other people dead on TV?" My mom is addicted to cop shows, and the plot lines are about as realistic as *The Lord of Rings* without elves.

"If that were true, I wouldn't have a job."

I closed my eyes and pictured Cindy the last time I'd seen her:

in her office, red-faced and arguing. Maybe I did know someone with a motive. David, Naomi's brother, had been furious with her. I'm sure it wouldn't improve my chances with her to give his name to the cops. But Cindy was dead. A second chance to get Naomi's number hardly mattered.

"There was a guy there—the new tenant. Cindy said she didn't want to give up, wanted to continue fighting to keep the bar. He got mad. I saw them arguing."

"Last name?"

"Beats me. But the landlord is Kevin Kearney, and he'll be able to tell you."

Cesar wrote the name down in the notebook he always carried—no digital notes for him—and slid the pad into his pocket. His calm, efficient manner reminded me that the gangly boy I'd known since childhood had chosen the perfect profession for himself. When we'd been together, I'd wanted to shield him from its demanding darkness. He'd always said, "Somebody's got to do it."

I shuddered. Now, I was glad that somebody was him.

"You all right?" The kettle whistled. He went to it and poured the hot water over my tea.

When the heat of the mug soaked into my palms, I answered. "Yeah. I'll be all right."

It wasn't the first time I'd seen a dead body, and I don't mean at funerals. I'd found my grandfather shot in the head in his grocery store on Mission Street my sophomore year of high school. Cesar had been with me. Futures had been forged that day—his vocation and mine, and the bond we never could shake.

"What was going on with Cindy? Relationship trouble? Money problems?"

"All of the above." I blew over the surface of my tea, staring into the vacant center of the room. "She had tons of debt, but it wasn't the sketchy loan-shark kind."

"Doesn't matter. Money problems make people desperate. Bad things can happen. What about relationships?"

"The trouble with the bar caused problems at home. She was killing herself trying to save it. And the money problems caused them tension, too."

"Was she depressed?"

"Yeah. Until last night when she got completely fired up again."

"Alma?" The office door squealed open, and Jenny Wong entered. "Are you okay?"

I nodded.

She glanced at Cesar. He nodded too, lying for me. I didn't hate him for that, although I resented that he knew I'd appreciate it.

"Jenny, this is Detective Cesar Garza. Cesar, this is—"

"Supervisor Wong." He stood and offered his hand. "Nice to meet you."

It would have been polite if I also stood, but my legs were made of tapioca at the moment.

"I heard about Cindy." Jenny's voice wavered as if she had a lump in her throat to match mine. Before her election, she was a high-profile civil rights lawyer with a focus on housing discrimination. She'd consulted with Cindy and me on legal issues in our fight to save The Carlos Club.

"Yes. I'm afraid she's dead." Cesar stood straight, like he wanted the Supervisor to have a good impression of him. It accentuated his lean height.

"Oh, my God." She stroked the skin of her throat. "What happened?"

I couldn't say how, but with an invisible sign only my subconscious recognized, Cesar signaled to me to keep quiet. How I found Cindy, the nature of her injuries—it was evidence he needed to keep under wraps.

He stepped forward. "We're investigating that right now. I'm just finishing up taking Reverend Lee's statement."

Reverend Lee? His formality stung. Like I hadn't lost my straight virginity to him. Like he hadn't refused to come to my ordination because organized religion is a scam. Like we didn't know each other as well as either of us knew anyone.

Then again, he said the department was understaffed, and he'd be stuck investigating the death of a fellow member of the Mission High class of 2006. Maybe he needed to maintain the appearance of professional distance.

Jenny drew a business card from her purse. "Call me if I can be of help. I assisted Cindy with her legal issues, and I can name everyone she's pissed off." She leaned closer. "I'd check out that reporter from *The City Weekly*. His smear campaign felt very personal."

No more than Cindy's smear campaign against her greedy

landlord, but pointing out the equivalence felt disloyal to my dead friend.

My junior warden turned to me. "Shall we skip morning prayer?"

I almost told her she could go ahead without me. Then I remembered our doorway was a crime scene. "Yes," I choked out. "Let's skip it today."

She grabbed my hand and gave it a squeeze. "Take care of yourself. This is a nasty shock."

I returned the pressure. "Thanks."

When she left, Cesar pulled out his notepad from his seat pocket and perched on the desk again. "What time did you leave the bar?"

"About ten."

He shook his head. "No abouts in a murder investigation."

I squeezed my eyes shut against the thought that I was being questioned. When I'd plugged my phone in to charge on my nightstand, I'd checked the time. "I was in bed by 10:26, so I definitely left before ten after. You know me—never scrimping on the oral hygiene—it takes at least six minutes to brush and floss thoroughly."

"Can anyone verify that?"

"My hygiene? I'm sure if you called my dentist—"

"Alma." My nickname had apparently gotten lost somewhere between Cindy's body and my office, even though Jenny had left us to continue our conversation in private.

"Are you asking if I came home alone?" Damn, if only I'd had a warm and willing Naomi with me to rub in his face.

"No. Yes." He grabbed a fistful of his coarse waves, mussing his part. "Not because I suspect you, but because I will need to record everyone's movements."

"I was alone."

Did his shoulders just relax an inch? Probably only my imagination. What did he care who I slept with? He'd dropped me and never looked back. Then again, I didn't give a damn who shared his bed, but I also didn't want any details.

"I saw that David guy leave with his sister ahead of me, but he could have come back—"

My phone buzzed in my pocket. Lynn, Cindy's wife. The knot of emotions lodged in my throat again, blocking my words.

I showed Cesar the screen.

He'd only met Lynn once, when we'd gone to their wedding as a couple, but he never forgot names.

"Right. I'll go break the news."

"I'll go with you." I braced myself for Cesar's argument. It didn't come.

He was staring out the door, watching the activity.

"You're okay with me coming along?"

He glanced up and shrugged. "She's going to need a shoulder to cry on."

And just like that, we were connected again.

Outside, Cesar paced the edge of the crime scene, now marked off with that yellow tape. A blanket covered Cindy's body. A man in a white, plastic clean suit snapped photos in the middle of the street.

Officers shared information with Cesar. I could have eavesdropped, if only my mind had knocked off its chant, *Cindy's dead. You left her alone.*

Chapter Three

When I didn't take her call, Lynn texted me.

Cindy didn't make it home. Isn't picking up. Did she crash on your couch?

Sleepovers on my sofa had been frequent when we'd been waging Operation Keep Carlos Open. Lynn worked night shifts in the ICU, so she didn't mind.

I ignored the message and the bubble of guilt, fear and panic that remained lodged in my throat. The news we brought needed to be said face to face. At the end of this car ride, I would explain that her wife of three years, her hopes of starting a family, the mother of their Dalmatian Fido was dead.

As Cesar drove across the Bay Bridge, fingers of fog floated over the water. On the new span, the elegant white sweep of the suspension cables shone bright in the morning glare.

Cesar slammed on the breaks two inches from the red lights ahead of us. Rush hour was a mess, even on the reverse commute to the East Bay.

"Why the hell do people move to Oakland, anyway?" he grumbled.

I didn't bother answering. He knew perfectly well how much cheaper housing was on the other side of the Bay. Thirteen months ago, he and Mario had shared an in-law apartment with rent control, mold, and zero sunlight. They probably still did.

"Who else will we need to notify? Parents, children, siblings?"

"*Nada*. Lynn is—was her only family."

"Right." His exhalation sounded an awful lot like a sigh of relief.

"So how does this work? Do you make a list of suspects? Search for the murder weapon? Find DNA evidence?" He'd only been a detective a few months when he'd dumped me, and we'd been too busy arguing to talk about our jobs.

"Yeah. It's just like on CSI."

"There's no need for sarcasm."

He didn't bother to apologize. "You realize that in addition to notifying Lynn about Cindy's death, I'll need to question her."

My shoulder muscles bunched. I had not in fact realized this was his plan, but it made sense. She might know something useful. "Yeah. Of course."

"Spouses are prime suspects."

Oh, that kind of questioning. I dug my fingernails into my knees.

"Lynn didn't do it." She couldn't murder anyone.

"I'm not going to argue with you. Just stay out of the way while I question her. I promise I'll be sensitive to her loss."

I snorted. "Sensitive to her loss? Was that the title of some in-service training you had—Five steps to appearing sensitive while secretly interrogating a suspect?"

I lowered the volume on his classic rock station.

He raised it again.

I dialed the nob to public radio.

He pressed the power button, leaving us in thick silence.

"If there's a trail of blood across Fourteenth Street, does that mean she crossed the road after she'd been hit?"

I watched his face and saw a telltale flinch.

"She was trying to get to me. For—" I choked on the word *help.*

"Maybe. Or just trying to run. We can't be sure."

He was hoping to make me feel better. It wasn't working.

"What did you find in the bar?"

"Booze. Stools. A jukebox."

I shot him a bird right next to his razor sharp cheekbone, so he didn't miss it with his gaze glued to the bridge. "Can you tell where she was attacked?"

"Alls, this is an active murder investigation. I can't reveal details." He flipped on the blinker and exited the highway. His GPS showed an ETA of nine minutes—the final countdown until I had to break the news to Lynn.

I flipped down the sun visor. "Have you done a death

notification before?"

"Yeah. But never somebody I knew. I'm glad you're here." He slid his hand off the wheel and brushed my outer thigh with his knuckles. Under different circumstances, the touch might have been flirtatious. Instead, it was chastely reassuring—a familiar caress to remind us both we were there for each other.

It took four rings of an emphatic doorbell before Lynn came to the front door in pink plaid pajamas, her sandy hair hanging in a loose ponytail. She looked from me to Cesar and back, a crease deepening between her brows. "What's going on?"

"Do you remember Cesar?"

She nodded, retreating into the dark house.

"Let's sit." I followed her in, steered her to a couch where Fido lay curled at one end.

She spoke as she lowered herself. "She's hurt isn't she? Was it a car accident?"

I crouched before her and locked onto her gaze. "She's dead, sweetie."

Lynn's cry sliced through the quiet room. Fido jumped off the couch and clawed for purchase on the hardwood floor.

I took the spot next to her as she cried and the dog whimpered.

Cesar remained straight and still in the doorway.

I stroked Lynn's back, feeling my grief seep out of me to join hers.

She gasped out a question. "What happened?"

"I fo—"

"Lynn, I promise I will do everything I can to find out."

She blinked at him. "You mean?"

"Cindy was murdered."

In my arms, she stiffened. A clock ticked in the next room. "A robbery?"

I shook my head. "No—"

"Everything is under investigation," Cesar said. "And I'll need to ask you some questions."

I shot eye darts at him.

He cleared his throat. "When you're ready, of course."

His phone rang, belting out a guitar riff and half the chorus of Def Leppard's "Pour Some Sugar on Me" before he silenced it.

Oh, sweet baby Jesus, had he skipped the class in detective school about silencing your ringer on the death notification? I was going to wring his neck when we got back into his car.

"Sorry," he muttered, retreating from my crazy-mad laser eyes. "I'll just take this in the kitchen and leave you two alone."

"I don't understand." Lynn sniffed, wiping her nose on her pink sleeve. "Who would want to kill Cindy?"

"I don't know." And I'd gotten the message that I wasn't supposed to reveal the details I knew.

"Are you helping him?"

I squeezed her hand. "I wanted to be here when you found out." Also, I apparently needed to convince him she was innocent.

She rose unsteadily and walked to a bar cart. She unscrewed a bottle of bourbon and poured some of its contents into a glass. I checked my watch. 9:45 a.m. But hey, it's five o'clock everywhere when you find out your wife has been murdered.

She downed the glass in one quick gulp. "Want one?"

My mind raced with memories of last night and this morning. An ounce of whatever she was pouring would calm my thoughts, but what if I missed something Cesar needed me to remember? "No thanks."

"You don't trust him, do you?" She'd dropped her voice to a whisper, barely audible over Cesar's side of a phone conversation in her kitchen.

Actually, I trusted him with pretty much anything aside from my heart and remembering to put his phone on vibrate. It had played "Highway to Hell" the one and only time he ever came to hear me preach and "Living on a Prayer" during Mario's police academy graduation ceremony.

"He's a hater, Alma. Have you forgotten the things he said to you? Total homophobe. He doesn't care about people like us."

Cesar was neither a hater nor a homophobe. He'd just taken issue with the fact that his girlfriend preferred to hang out in the dyke bar when she wasn't with him. I'd always been more than he could handle and had refused to shrink down to a simpler version of myself so he could accept me.

"Promise me you'll stick to him. Make sure he does right by Cindy."

"He will." Cesar was very by-the-book, one of our many problems as a couple.

Open relationship—no.

Domestic partnership instead of marriage—no.

That had been our first breakup. We'd been so young, right out of college. I'd sown some wild oats, Cesar tried to find a girl much nicer and more ordinary than me.

The next time we got together, gay marriage was legal, I heartily approved of the institution, and I'd learned that as much as I'd tried to be otherwise—I was a one-human girl, a monogamist by nature. Even my newfound conventionality hadn't been enough to make us work.

Cesar's low voice rumbled in the kitchen. "David Cohen. 135 Abbey. Got it. I'm headed straight there."

So suspect *numero uno* lived on a mid-block alley, the other side of Dolores from St. Giles' and The Carlos Club. If I wanted to track down Naomi, I'd have to start at his place.

Did I want to, if her brother had murdered my friend?

Lynn drew her knees up onto the couch, a barrier between us. "Cindy told me you argued last night."

I jerked my gaze to hers. "I thought you didn't talk to her."

"That was the last time. A little after ten. I was on a break at work. She was spitting mad that you were giving up."

"I know. But it was time, Lynn."

"It was time a year ago. Two even. If she'd quit on The Carlos Club, we'd still have some savings. Maybe we'd have a baby by now. And she wouldn't be…"

The word hung in the air. Fido whimpered again. Whoever said Dalmatians are a dumb breed hadn't recognized their gift for subtext.

Lynn scratched him under his chin, tears streaming down her face. "I know, boy. I know."

Apparently, this was the moment for voicing regrets. "I shouldn't have left her last night. I should have stayed. Seen the party to its end. Tucked her in on my sofa so she could sleep off her rum and cokes."

"Had she drunk a lot of those?" Cesar had slinked into the room, quiet as a panther, and I hadn't even noticed.

I drew my feet up under me, still laced up past my ankles in my burgundy combat boots. At the moment shoes on the sofa were the least of Lynn's concern, and it took forever to untie the damn things. Next time, I was buying a pair with zippers.

"I don't know how many she'd had, but she wasn't very steady on her feet when she climbed atop the bar to give a speech. And booze tends… tended to shorten her fuse."

Cesar glanced at Lynn, who nodded in confirmation.

"Would this be a good time to ask you some questions?" Cesar had his notebook ready, like a waiter anticipating an order.

Lynn's reply dripped acid. "What do you think?"

He flinched—not that anyone who hadn't spent hours admiring his features would have noticed. Poor Cesar. He'd had to trek across the Bay Bridge—a journey San Franciscans loathed like a redeye to New Jersey—to get sassed by an uncooperative widow he was trying to help.

I laid my hand on one of her socked feet. "I don't think it will ever feel like a good time. But anything you can tell Cesar now will help while the trail is fresh."

I raised my brows, silently asking him if that last part was true, or a cliché I'd picked up from Mama's cop shows.

He scowled but nodded. I could practically hear his thoughts. *She thinks she knows how to do my job from watching TV.*

So far, so true. I grinned.

"Alma mentioned Cindy got in money trouble over the bar."

"She spent everything and borrowed tons." Eyes closed, Lynn stroked Fido's head. Her hollow tone was neither sad nor angry, which seemed odd. Shouldn't she be one or the other?

"Standard business loans from the bank or personal loans?" Cesar asked.

Lynn opened her eyes, frowning at him. "As far as I know, all totally legit."

"Would you say she had any enemies?"

"She and the landlord have been at each other's throats, and that reporter at *The City Weekly* was fanning the flames. If Kearney got what he was asking for the place from the new tenant, he'll make another sixty K next year."

Sixty thousand was a lot of money to Cindy, but it was a drop in Kevin Kearney's deep bucket. He owned commercial real estate all over the city. The fight had been ideological to him as much as it had been for Cindy and me.

Still, Cesar was scribbling notes, not ruling him out as a suspect, so I added him to my mental list. Thinking about who had done it and why quelled the choking, guilty panic trying to rise up my throat.

He glanced up at her again. "Did she drive to the city last

night?"

"No. Her transmission died last month and we can't afford to fix it. I picked her up when I wasn't working. Or she slept at Alma's. Or she took the Transbay bus."

"And last night?"

"I expected her to stay at Alma's, until she told me they'd argued. That's the only reason I was surprised when I got home from work and she wasn't here."

"What time was that?"

"7:20 or so. I work the seven to seven shift."

"And where's that?"

"Tate Heights Medical Center. I'm an ICU nurse."

Cesar put his pencil behind his ear, which somehow only made him look sexy, when ninety-nine percent of people would have looked like a big ol' geek accessorized like that.

"Thanks, Lynn. I appreciate you answering these questions right now. It helps a lot. Alma will stay here to keep you company while I hit the pavement."

What? He was dumping me in the East Bay? That would leave me with a sixty-dollar taxi fare or two hours on public transportation. On a different day, I might have said, *over my dead body.*

But it was Cindy's dead body in question, and she wouldn't have been dead if I'd been a better friend. The only thing I could do for Lynn and Fido was to make sure Cesar found her murderer, and he certainly wouldn't let me tag along to interview David Cohen. I may as well ditch him and find my own way to corner suspect *numero uno.* At least Cesar seemed less suspicious of Lynn.

"See you later." I wriggled into the cushion next to the widow and her dog like I planned to stay there for a long time.

He narrowed his eyes at me. Damn. I must seem too compliant. I shot him a bird for good measure.

His shoulders relaxed, and he made for the door. "Lynn, I'm sorry about Cindy."

"Thanks, Cesar. That means a lot." She flipped him off, too.

He sighed and, chuckling, showed himself out.

I sat with Lynn as she called her parents, then her sister Marie in L.A. Marie began packing while they talked, preparing to make the drive.

After Lynn's telephone calls, she closed her eyes and dropped her head to rest on the back of the sofa. "What's next?"

"When the coroner releases the body, I'll help you with the arrangements. Do you think she would have wanted a service?"

"Yes. She'd want you to do it."

"Okay. Then we'll take care of that, too. But right now—"

"I want to pop a Valium and sit here."

"Personally, I'm a big believer in the comfort of binge-watching television. Did you know you can stream all eight seasons of *Will and Grace*?"

This was a point of contention between Jordan, my friend from seminary, and me. When she'd been heartbroken, knocked up, and dumped, I'd forced her into a *Vicar of Dibley* marathon. Somehow it had earned me a reputation for callous pastoral care.

Clearly, Jordan underestimated the healing power of T.V. in general and cheesy sitcoms in particular.

Lynn, however, did not. "Oh my God, please turn that on and make sure it won't stop until my sister gets here."

I complied. She put her head on my shoulder, and I stroked her hair until she dozed on the couch. As I watched the sitcom, my thoughts snagged on her odd tone when she'd told Cesar about Cindy accruing debt. Had Lynn been lying about something, or trying to lead us in a certain direction?

Perhaps she'd just gone numb. Too bad Cesar had left and taken his expertise with him. I had no clue what counted as normal for someone in Lynn's situation.

Mom called me around lunchtime. She'd heard the news. She and Dad only lived six blocks from St. Giles'. I took the call in the kitchen.

"Are you okay, *mija*?"

Was I? The lump in my throat hadn't budged all morning. But Cesar had been right. Alma Lee is not allowed to get hysterical.

"Yeah, Mom, *estoy bien*."

"I'm so sorry about your friend. I always liked her hair."

I laughed, then swallowed it quickly so Lynn wouldn't hear.

"Are her parents still in the neighborhood? Your father and I would like to send a basket." Mom was the genius behind Lee's Gourmet Gift Baskets, which she now shipped nation-wide.

Her offer filled my chest with warmth, making me aware of just how cold I'd been.

"No. Growing up, it was only her dad. He died a few years ago. But thanks for the thought. You could send one to her wife." I gave Mom Lynn's address and begged off the phone.

"Take care, *mija.*"

"You too, Mama." I ended the call.

Chapter Four

I stayed with Lynn, forcing her to drink water and eat chocolate until her sister arrived from L.A. In the late afternoon, I greeted Marie and handed over the care of my friend.

It was 4:00 p.m. Surely Cesar had been and gone from David Cohen's house by then. I took BART back to the Mission.

On the train, the businessman across from me held the print edition of the Chronicle open. The cover featured a photo of Jenny Wong in a shimmering blue sequined dress accepting a thick glass ornament. *Rising political star Wong accepts the 'Friend of Families Award' at Charity Gala,* read the headline.

I hadn't found Cindy's body early enough for her murder to make print. Would it be Saturday's lead story?

Would Cesar have solved the case by then? Perhaps David had left a bloody fingerprint at the crime scene.

Or maybe Lynn had, said the devil's advocate who lived in my brain and happened to sound exactly like Cesar.

Impossible. She was at work. It had to be David.

When I came up from the station, I texted Cesar. *Any news?*

Not for nosy members of the public.

But I'm a friend of the victim.

He sent me a middle finger emoji, which was no less than I deserved for flashing the same at him earlier in the flesh. He'd taken the time to choose the brown one that best matched his complexion. Good for him.

I made straight for Abbey Street and climbed the steps to a baby blue Victorian with two units. The entry on the right read 135. I rang the bell, just under a mezuzah nailed to the doorframe.

Footsteps alerted me someone approached from the other side. The door opened to reveal Naomi, paler than she'd been last night. She pressed her lips tight before she spoke. "What are you doing here?"

Shit. I had a plan to confront David, and it didn't start this way.

"Is your brother here?"

"They took him down to the station for questioning." Tears filled her lower lids, then spilled down her cheeks.

My stomach twisted.

She wiped her face with the back of her hand. "I'm sorry about your friend, but David would never do that. He couldn't. And he was here all night after we got home."

A thousand questions sprang to mind, like I was a natural-born interrogator. But more loudly my lizard brain screamed, *Pretty girl crying! Hug her!* After a moment of confusion, I determined it was time to make and then implement Plan B by harnessing both of these powerful instincts.

"You must be worried. Can I come in, so you can tell me all about it?"

Her lips pursed, but her shoulders fell. A little more persuasion, and she'd be swinging the door wide open.

"I've known Cindy since high school. She was one of my oldest friends."

Naomi's wary expression softened, but the door didn't budge.

Evidence of the presence of children littered the stairwell. A pair of tiny rain boots and a matching umbrella. A limp plush monkey lay prone on the carpet next to an empty shoe shelf. Something about the toy tightened my ribs.

"Your brother has kids?"

She nodded. "Aviva's three, and there's a baby on the way."

"Was she here when the detective came?" Hopefully Cesar could manage that with more tact than he'd handled Lynn. As the oldest of five, he was great with kids, wanted to make as many little Garzas as his parents had.

"No." The door creaked open an inch. "Melissa took Aviva to her parents' in New Jersey a few days ago. David's been here alone, perseverating over his plans." Bitterness edged her words.

Or was that the acrid scent suddenly pouring down the stairs? Smoke. As soon as I thought the word. An alarm blared—one of those new-fangled and extremely loud ones with a robot voice shouting, "Fire! Fire!"

"Dammit." She bolted up the stairs.

A fire wasn't exactly the invitation I'd been waiting for, but I seized the opportunity and followed her in the direction of the smoke. In the kitchen, she opened the oven. Gray clouds billowed out. She fanned them with a dishtowel, and I opened all the windows, grabbing an issue of the New Yorker to beat the eye-stinging fumes outside.

One alarm in another room quieted so that only the device directly overhead bellowed at us. The stupid thing was loud enough to make my heart race even though I knew there was no actual fire.

Naomi pulled a casserole pan out of the oven. Blackened bubbles covered the surface of what she'd been cooking.

"Damn broiler."

She might just as easily have damned me, the uninvited caller interrupting her cooking.

"What was it?" I asked, hoping to distract her from that inconvenient truth.

"Kugel. Comfort food for David." And then she started to cry right into the Pyrex pan full of ash.

Hug her! screamed my lizard brain, far louder than the fire alarm had been. *But she didn't even invite me in,* I rationalized with those base instincts too stupid to grasp reason. *She only tolerated me following her in the role of volunteer-firefighter.*

Still, she was new in town, her brother was being questioned at the police station. She needed a friend. I went to her side and stood close enough to let our arms touch.

She leaned into me. My ribs squeezed my heart tight. I wanted to hold her and let her cry on my shoulder, the mysterious beauty wearing a bracelet with a verse from the Song of Songs. But since I'd been putting the moves on her last night, I opted for standing firm like a pillar instead.

What a mess. Someone had killed Cindy, and it was going to devastate a lot of other people's lives. This is what people don't understand about sin. It's not an action that puts you on Santa and God's naughty list, or gets you damned to hell. It's a single choice, often thoughtless, that harms countless others—usually the ones you love most. And then you have to live with it forever.

God always forgives; usually it's people who can't.

If David killed Cindy in a moment of rage, it would devastate Naomi and his family, as well as Lynn and the family she'd wanted.

And me—I'd be staring across Fourteenth Street every day, wondering if I might have saved Cindy's life, if only I'd been less petulant at that damn party.

Naomi sucked in a deep breath and grabbed a spatula, digging under the blackened layer of her casserole to reveal creamy noodles baked together.

Hey look, a bright side. "It's probably edible."

She sighed. "It'll taste like a bonfire."

My stomach chose that moment to grumble. She quirked her brow, the one with the scar. So cute the way it arched over her glasses. Almost as cute as the gap between her front teeth.

"Hungry for a bonfire, are you?"

Along with Lynn, I'd eaten nothing but chocolate all day. She'd devoured a bag of Hershey's miniatures and dug out a bar of vegan, fair trade organic with 70% cacao for me. Just like the TV binging, allowing her to eat only candy would not meet my friend Jordan's pastoral care standards. But hey, everybody has their own style. And when Jordan was pregnant, I cooked her vegan feasts while she snuck milkshakes behind my back, the traitor. So sue me if I opted for pastoral chocolate these days.

"I'm hungry in general, I think." And that noodle kugel definitely wasn't vegan. "How about I throw something together for us? Or we could get out of here…?"

She glanced around. "I want to be here when David comes back."

"Okay. Permission to rummage through your fridge?"

"Sure. But you won't find much."

I opened the french double doors of the refrigerator. She was right. Its shelves were bare. But my dad had taught me you can always make a stir-fry with the last random vegetables in the produce drawer. One rib of celery, two carrots, and a gorgeous bunch of broccolini. Of course, garlic and… "Do you have ginger?"

"I think there's some in the freezer."

Perfect. Just where it belonged.

I set rice to cook in David's Instant Pot. It would not meet the standards of my father's kitchen, but it worked okay for white people.

As I chopped veggies, I admired the hydroponic herb garden in the windowsill, with a beta fish to fertilize it. Mason jars full of liquids of various colors filled the fridge door. I pulled one out and held it up to the light.

"Fruit shrubs for mixing drinks," Naomi said. "Melissa hates them."

Magnets affixed notecards to the fridge with what appeared to be color-coded cocktail recipes. Green for gin drinks, blue for vodka, bourbon and whisky on the pink cards, and tequila on the yellow.

As the oil heated in the frying pan, I skimmed through the cards. His recipes sounded damn good. *Gin, Fernet, orange juice, maple syrup and lemon juice, served on the rocks. He'd called it The Last Hope.*

"He's a software engineer, but only because my parents made him get his degree. All he's ever wanted to be was a bartender, ever since he worked at a bar back in high school. His wife didn't mind the idea until she realized the hours would leave her home alone with Aviva most nights and weekends."

A bottle of prenatal vitamins stood in the windowsill. "I guess Melissa left these."

Naomi rubbed her eyes. "She's five months along. It's a boy."

When we sat to eat, still and facing each other for the first time since our almost-kiss, her captivating lips pulled wide and taut—the grimace of sympathy. "I'm sorry about your friend."

"Yeah. Me too." I pinched a chunk of carrot between disposable chopsticks she'd found in David's miscellany drawer. It was too hot, but I choked it down along with the lump in my throat.

"I know David seemed angry. He's just really stressed about opening the bar. It's his dream. He took out a second mortgage on this condo, and… um, his marriage is strained… "

I let her talk, drawn by both her concern for her brother and desperation to learn something that might shed light on who hurt my friend. Plan B was working.

"You said David was here all night. Did you sleep over?"

"I'm crashing here until I find a place for myself."

"Is it possible he left while you were sleeping?"

She scooted her vegetables around on her plate, sorting them into piles. "Sure, it's possible. But it's unlikely. I'm a light sleeper, and he's a total klutz."

"And that's what you told the police?"

"I might have been more emphatic." She smiled sheepishly—a loyal sister—and popped a broccolini floret into her mouth. "Oh, my God. This is so good."

What can I say? I'm a woman of many talents. "I'm glad you like it."

She glanced at her watch, chewing even though I was nearly certain she'd already swallowed her bite.

"How long ago did the cops take David?"

"Hours. I called a lawyer. He's there with him, and he's texted me a few times, but it's been a while. He says it's important for David to cooperate."

Well damn. They must have something seriously incriminating on him. As if the same thought occupied us both, we ate in silence.

When she cleared her plate, she dabbed at the corners of that gorgeous mouth with a cloth napkin, which showed a commendable concern for the environment.

"I hate to ask you this about your friend, but do you think it could have been random? Or a robbery? Or does someone have a real motive to kill her? Because David…"

"Cindy could be exasperating, but I don't think anyone wanted to kill her for it. And I heard the cops say she still had her phone and wallet when they were examining her."

"You were there?"

The lump swelled in my throat like I'd swallowed a whole bulb of garlic. "I found her. She was on the steps of the church. I think she crawled there after the attack."

Behind her glasses, the worry in Naomi's eyes softened to compassion.

"I walked out on her last night after she argued with your brother. The idea of fighting for her lease was ridiculous, and I got mad. But now it seems so petty."

The doorbell rang. She shot out of her seat and thumped down the stairs.

I cleared our plates.

"Oh, hi. Is David here?" An airy voice floated up from downstairs—a woman, sounding young and confused.

"Sorry, no. Can I tell him you stopped by?"

Cesar didn't call me a nosy member of the public for no reason.

I sped down the stairs and tried to look casual as I hovered on the last step.

"Where is he?" The woman stepped closer, trying to peer around Naomi. "He hasn't replied to my texts all day."

"Something urgent came up." Naomi moved to fill the entire doorway. I came to her side to help.

The statuesque young woman sported the careless casual of the Mission hipster—oversized sweater, vintage sunglasses pushed up on her forehead, tight jeans of an awkward length neither capri nor ankle. The way she wore the outfit seemed wrong. Perhaps it was her stiff posture, or the fact that a sheath dress or a pair of wide-legged trousers would flatter her figure better.

Since I am the genuine article—Mission District born and raised—I didn't have to try so hard. I wore snug but comfortable black jeans, and my burgundy faux leather motorcycle jacket zipped up to hide my clerical collar.

She gave me a quick, puzzled glance, then refocused on Naomi. "Is he okay?"

"He should tell you that himself. Who should I say dropped by?"

"I'm Christina. Do you know if he's going to services with you tomorrow?"

"Nice to meet you, Christina." Naomi said the words without sounding even a little pleased. "I'll give your message to David as soon as I see him." She closed the door in the woman's face.

When she glanced at me, my eyes must have been huge. She giggled, then slapped her hand over her mouth. We dashed upstairs and let the laughter out at the top.

"Who the hell is Christina?"

"I don't know for sure, but considering how often she texts my brother, I assume she is at least half the reason Melissa left."

"Oh damn." That made Aviva's face-plant monkey even sadder.

"I feel the same way. Plus, I'm genuinely concerned my mother will murder him in his sleep." She reached for a bottle of whiskey and popped the cork with one thumb, pouring it into a glass, neat.

"No sage and blackberry for you?" I tapped one of the pink cards.

She winked. "Don't worry, the only thing I like straight is my whiskey." She downed the whole glass in one sip and blew out a breath.

My body heated like I'd just taken a fiery shot of booze.

"What are your marriage stats?"

I was single, obviously, or I wouldn't have been trying it on with her last night.

She set the glass down with a thud. "Have you hitched together any adulterers?"

Oh, right. The marriages I'd officiated.

"Not that I know of, although I'm working with a polyamorous couple to write a blessing service that isn't actually a marriage."

"Gotta love San Francisco." She poured herself more whiskey. "Want one?"

"Sure." As she poured, I studied her face, wanting to kiss the pink that had risen high on her cheeks and across her nose, wanting to know every single thing in addition to whiskey that brought the color to her face—embarrassment, laughter, tears? "Sometimes it seems like you know an awful lot about my job."

"Maybe." She shrugged.

"*L'Chaim*, Rabbi Cohen."

"*L'Chaim*, Reverend Lee." A smile played on her lips before she raised the glass to them and took a modest sip. "It took you long enough, by the way."

I sputtered. "That's not fair. You had like a million more clues to make your elementary little deduction."

"Excuses, excuses." She laughed, and her eyes twinkled.

My chest went tight with certainty. I'd just met my soul mate—sexy, smart, and spiritual. And best of all, Naomi would understand the pull of a vocation, the limitless duties of my job, the joy of pastoring people through their happiest highs and deepest valleys. Now we just needed to deal with the fact that her brother might have murdered Cindy.

Chapter Five

In the middle of Thursday night, the lump in my throat grew so big I considered trying to do the Heimlich maneuver on myself. I woke up on Friday determined to write my sermon. It was technically my day off, which just meant I didn't wear my collar when I went into the office or visited a parishioner. As the priest-in-charge of St. Giles', appointed by the bishop, I was too busy to carve a whole day out for myself. And how would I keep myself occupied if I played hooky on Fridays? Everything I loved to do fell under the umbrella of my work. I looked forward to hospital calls, diocesan meetings, and writing sermons.

However, it turns out it's hard to write a sermon when all you can think about is who murdered your friend. I wasted the entire day on six false starts, my mind constantly trying to draw me into amateur detection. Part of me wanted David Cohen to be guilty, so Cesar could wrap things up for Lynn. Hopefully, a resolution would also prevent me from choking to death on my own feelings.

The part of me smitten with Naomi wanted the culprit to be somebody else. But who?

That was Cesar's question to puzzle over for the moment, because the one I needed to ask was, *What the hell should I say Sunday morning from the pulpit of St. Giles?*

Eventually I gave up and went for a walk. Inspiration never failed me on the streets of my neighborhood. Only, this time, it did. My muse must have been napping at the morgue with Cindy's body.

By Saturday afternoon, I'd grown desperate. I called my very together friend Lily. She'd married a hot surfer and never procrastinated on her sermon so she could hang out with him on Saturdays.

"Any brilliant ideas on this passage in Matthew?"

"Honestly, I don't think you should touch the Gospel reading. Your text for tomorrow is the fact someone murdered a person on your doorstep."

The lump swelled even larger. Was I developing a goiter? Mental note: quit cooking with the natural sea salt and eat iodized Morton's with a spoon for lunch.

"She's your friend from the bar across the street, isn't she?"

"Yeah. I've known her since high school."

"Was it gang violence or a robbery?"

Lily hadn't grown up in the city, and she lived in her husband's mansion in the rolling hills of the St. Francis Wood neighborhood. I tried not to bristle at her assumptions about my neck of an entirely different woods.

"No. The police don't think so."

"Well, if it related to her fight to keep the bar, then you point out how far the powers that be will go to silence the marginalized."

See, Lily's not so bad. She gets it big time even though she married her sugar daddy. And I don't blame her—the man has abs like Batman and worships every square of sidewalk she walks on.

"The problem is—I can whip them up into frenzy, but what's the goal? I'm certainly not going to pick up Cindy's torch." Parish priest, community organizer, nosy citizen—I already spread myself too thin. Bar proprietor would break this camel's back.

"No. A frenzy is not a good idea. What's your call to action after this tragedy? Comfort each other? Take to the streets to protest violence?"

I pictured Cindy's blazing eyes, her gaping mouth—the fury she'd fired at me the last time I'd seen her alive.

"I want them to get right with each other, to make peace and resolve conflicts. That's the way to resist violence."

"That'll preach. Go with it."

"Thanks, Lil." I ended the call and cranked out a thousand words in an hour. As I was reading through the text, someone knocked on my door.

One of the liabilities of living adjacent to the church—people dropped by all the time. I peeked through the window. Jenny Wong, Supervisor of the 9th District and my junior warden stood outside in a navy-blue power suit. I zipped up my hoodie to hide my lack of a bra and opened the door.

When she'd been elected, I thought for sure she would resign from the time-consuming demands of parish leadership, but she'd laughed me off. "Coffee hour is my only social life. Morning Prayer feeds my soul. I'm going to be here anyway, so I may as well keep helping out." And thank God she had. Not only did she share my work ethic (which Lily called poor boundaries), but she was an invaluable mentor.

"Hey, how are you holding up?" The concern in her voice sloughed off layers of the calluses I'd been trying to build since yesterday, leaving me stinging and raw in my doorway.

"I'm okay. Working on my sermon."

"Good, good. That can't be easy, after…"

"No. It's not. Come on in." I swept my arm, reiterating the invitation.

As she entered, she shook her head. "Poor Cindy."

"Yeah." I coughed, trying to clear the lump from my throat.

"She was such a fighter, right up to the end." Her distant, hollow tone matched my mood.

I dropped onto my sofa. "If she'd only learned to quit the fights she couldn't win, she might still be alive."

"Maybe so, but I can't entirely blame her." Jenny sat in the armchair. "If I beat Alvarez in the upcoming election, it will be by the skin of my teeth, but I'm not going to give up."

"Really?" I'd assumed her reelection was a given, with her tangible progress on affordable housing. She was a darling of the newspaper, scoring a glowing headline nearly every week, while I'd barely heard a thing about her opponent.

"He's buddies with Camilla Ferris." The former district attorney recently won a national senate seat. "And he's courting the mayor, whose support I cannot afford to lose." She squeezed her eyes shut and pinched the bridge of her nose, then sucked in a big breath and looked at me. "I didn't drop by to talk about the never-ending battle for reelection. You realize you left us waiting at El Sinaloense for our warden's lunch yesterday?"

"Crap." I'd been at Lynn's, and my standing date with the chairs of St. Giles' governing committee had escaped my mind. Not smart, since they were effectively my bosses. "Don't hesitate to text me if I'm not where I'm supposed to be." Sadly, it happened more than I wanted to admit.

"I didn't want to bother you after everything—"

"Still, I'm so sorry I didn't cancel. I went over to Oakland with Detective Garza when he made the death notification. As ad hoc police chaplain, I guess you could say." A pathetic excuse, considering how busy Jenny was.

"I figured it was something like that. I told Al what happened. He was very distressed and came straight over to make sure everything was cleaned up properly."

When I'd come back from David's after dinner with Naomi, the sidewalk had been scrubbed clean. I'd just assumed the police had done it. I'd thank Al tomorrow at church.

"You should know, he wasn't thrilled to learn about it from me. He thought you should have called your senior warden right away with news like that."

Fair enough, but he should have told me himself. I squeezed a foam football that I kept on my desk for whenever a parishioner tried to triangulate me. "I'm sorry to hear he felt out of the loop. It would be really helpful if you'd encourage him to tell me directly about his frustration."

"Oh, I know." She waved away my concern. "I nudged him your way. But you know how he is…"

I did. Opinionated as hell, a tad conflict averse, but as devoted to the parish as Jenny.

"You know—" She dropped onto my couch. "After you were late to the finance committee last week, and then you decided to read that sermon from Martin Luther King instead of writing one yourself, Al's a bit stirred up. He thinks you're not focused on your job, you don't do enough pastoral care, you aren't ever in the office."

"You can't do pastoral care only in the office." A dull ache throbbed behind my eyes. I closed them and gently pressed my thumbs against my lids, then opened them to add, "You have to go to where the sheep are."

"Hey, you're preaching to the choir." She held up both her palms. "But, Al can't carry a tune, so to speak. And he has a rector mold in his head that you couldn't fill no matter how hard you tried."

It probably had a penis and two-point-five kids or a bouffant of grandma hair and a matronly bosom.

The bishop had appointed me vicar of St. Giles' a year and a half ago. We'd shared the high hopes that if the parish could become financially sound, they would hire me as their rector. The congregation was doing well on the money side, but apparently I wasn't rector-shaped enough for Al.

I dropped onto the sofa next to Jenny, slumping and letting my legs splay wide. "Well, if Al decides to speak directly to me about his concerns, I will let him know I spent the whole of Thursday ministering to the victim's family."

"He might ask you if she's a pledging member before he counts that in your favor."

Ugh. Why didn't people like Al recognize that churches only grow when you focus outward, on the folks who don't yet belong? As soon as St. Giles' had started growing, the long-time members got antsy that they weren't getting enough of my attention.

"Want some tea?" A steaming cup of gunmetal green might shake me out of my funk.

"No thanks, I've got a rally at the hospital this afternoon, then a fundraiser for Senator Thacker to attend."

"Your schedule is relentless."

"Yep." She yawned, so I did too. Only, afterward, she remained bright-eyed, and I wanted to curl up on my couch and sleep until Tuesday.

"Thanks for the heads up about Al, and for your efforts to re-frame his perspective. I'm lucky to have you on my team."

"You're doing a great job, Alma." She patted my knee, then stood. "Sundays are so joyful since you came to St. Giles'. Al will come along, I promise. We just have to help him see the big picture."

"Yeah. I'm sure you're right."

Once Jenny left, I sat at my computer to tighten up the sermon. With its focus on Cindy's death, tomorrow morning wasn't likely to be joyful in the least.

Chapter Six

As I fine-tuned my sermon, I remembered an article the paper published about Cindy a few months earlier. I found it online, scrolled through it, and cringed at a quote. "Kevin Kearney is what's wrong with San Francisco. He evicts grandmas, raises the rent on struggling families and doesn't give a damn about the traditional populations who've taken refuge in this city for decades."

The newspapers' site linked to a follow-up article with a video clip. In it, Kevin Kearney stood in a conference room somewhere, behind a podium with a white and blue Kearney Properties logo on it. Those fluorescent lights were not kind to his fading strawberry blond hair.

"The Carlos Club is a blight on the neighborhood. Its clientele are the wrong sort of people for the new Mission, and its proprietor couldn't turn a profit selling snow cones in hell." He laughed at his own joke.

I'd wanted to punch him the first time I'd seen it. Now that Cindy was dead, I might go for a kick to the groin instead.

Were the police looking into him, or did they have enough evidence to charge David Cohen? Cesar would never tell me, so I may as well ask the guy myself.

I texted Naomi. *Is your brother home?*

Came home at 3 a.m. and went straight to bed.

My thumbs flew over the screen. *Good. Let me bring you two takeout.*

Really? That would be awesome.

Damn. This subterfuge might come back to bite me later. I

called in an order to the falafel place down the street and glanced outside.

Those bright blue skies could be deceptive. It looked warm, but in early June they meant I should trade out my vegan leather soldier jacket for a puffy down parka.

Sure enough, the day was frigid as only summer in San Francisco can be. Gales came barreling over the city from the ocean, blowing off the fog and turning Sixteenth Street into an arctic wind tunnel.

I'd almost reached Abbey Street, falafel in hand, when I skidded to a halt. My frozen brain had started working again, and it wanted to know what the hell I was doing. Al had indirectly dressed me down for spreading myself too thin, and I was off to stick my nose deeper into Cindy's murder.

Phenomenal plan, Alls. Maybe you should drop off the falafel and run.

Outside Garfield's coffee shop I gazed inside, but really, I searched the reflection of my own shadowy silhouette in the glass. Should I be Al's timely meeting attender and provider of insular pastoral care, or keep letting the spirit carry me wherever it wanted?

And, as ever, my reflection provided me with no answer. Without one, it was easy to continue to go with the flow, which always led me to the most interesting places.

And why not poke around about the case? Cesar said I was too nosy for my own good. But if you want to be helpful, to rally people, to show them how to make a difference, you've got to know what's going on.

On the other hand, I was no Miss Marple, or even that badass priest/helicopter pilot in those mystery novels everyone in seminary read. What was her name? Oh, right, Clare Fergusson. If Cesar found out, he'd rage at me like he had in the good old days, before he got too fed up with me to bother shouting anymore.

I really, really shouldn't feel all tingly inside at the prospect. But hey, they were my good old days for a reason.

And of course, I wanted to atone for my neglect of Cindy and honor Lynn's request. I wasn't snapping to attention because of Naomi.

I could imagine Cindy's cackle in my ear. *Nice try. It's totally about the girl. But I won't hold it against you.*

The bunched-up muscles of my throat relaxed for the first time since I'd seen her body. Had she just sprinkled mercy on me from above?

I turned onto Abbey and rang the bell.

David answered. Dark circles hung under his eyes like something perfectly round had punched both sides of his face.

"Yeah?" His gaze held no recognition we'd met.

"Hi, I'm Alma." I stuck out my hand, simultaneously hoisting the takeout bag. "I'm here to see Naomi. I brought food."

"Oh, right. She said you were coming."

He gave my hand a limp squeeze, then stepped aside. The shoe rack now housed Naomi's black Mary Janes and a pair of men's leather slide-ons.

"Come on up."

Above, the apartment seemed unnaturally quiet. The monkey was no longer lying face down in the entryway. I climbed the stairs.

"Hey." At the end of the dark, narrow hallway, Naomi stood in the bright kitchen, drying her hands on a dishtowel.

I passed closed doors and entered the cluttered, cozy room. A rich aroma filled the air—baking butter—the glorious scent of temptation. Despite sitting at the back of the flat, the kitchen was clearly the center of activity. As it should be. Had that been true when Melissa and Aviva were home? I shoved the sad thought aside.

"Hey, yourself." I stood a meter from Naomi, not sure how to greet her—a hug, a smooch on the cheek, a body-smashed-together kiss with lots of tongue? Planting my feet, I waited for a cue.

She gestured toward a chair. "Have a seat."

Well, that was definitely the least desirable option. I dropped my butt in the chair. Its hard slats slammed against my sit bones.

"So they didn't charge him?" I asked in a near-whisper.

She lifted one brow, shaking her head. "David, come tell Alma all about it. She wants to know if the police think you're a murderer."

Okay. So she'd ferreted me out in two seconds flat. Hopefully the falafel would win me her forgiveness.

David entered and sat across from me, elbows on the table, chin on his knuckles, as if the weight of his head was too much to carry. Was that the burden of guilt for bludgeoning my friend to death?

43

The lump in my throat re-formed.

"Tell her about the keys," Naomi said.

He unfolded and refolded a paper napkin. "So, when the police were questioning me, they kept asking me about keys. Had I received keys to The Carlos Club? Where were they now? They'd ask me where I was, how much was in my bank accounts, where Melissa and Aviva were. Then, always, they'd drop another question about these keys to the bar."

I leaned an inch closer to him over the table. "They found them at the crime scene?"

"Yeah. That's what they said. Somewhere inside the club." He blinked, as if nodding required too much strength.

It wasn't so weird to find a set of keys inside the building they opened. "Were they Cindy's or one of the bar tender's?"

Naomi tapped her fingers on the table. "Come on, the cops would have ruled that out."

Oh, right. See what I mean? I'm so not Miss Marple.

David twisted in the chair and grabbed something off the countertop. He dangled a ring with a single Schlage key and a square, white fob. It read *Kearney Properties*.

"The thing is, I did receive a ring identical to the one they found. It arrived by courier on Thursday morning, the first day of my lease on the bar, before I heard what happened to that woman."

"Cindy. Her name was Cindy."

He winced. "Sorry. Of course. Naomi mentioned she was your friend."

The simple acknowledgement softened me toward him. Even if they weren't his keys, it didn't prove him innocent. But it might implicate someone else—namely a greedy son of a bitch named Kevin Kearney. Was David suggesting the same thing?

I studied the bruised bags under his eyes, the tension in his mouth. He caught me looking and pulled a tight smile.

Naomi opened the oven and drew out a sheet of cookies. The source of the glorious-yet-taboo aroma. No cows should have to live in tiny stalls hooked up to pumping machines so I could eat buttery cookies. Plus, their farts account for 4.2% of greenhouse gasses.

"So." She spun and leaned against the counter, wielding a spatula. "Let's head over to Kearny Properties and learn who else had a key." She scraped the cookies off the sheet. Chocolate chip, by the looks of them. Doubly easy to refuse. I only eat vegan, fair trade chocolate, and I'd have put money on those being Tollhouse morsels.

"Are they open on Saturday?" I asked.

"Yeah," David said, "But why would they talk to us?"

She wagged the spatula at him. "Because you are a very upset new tenant, shocked that a murder has taken place on the property and offended that you've become a suspect because of their key chain gone astray."

"That could backfire big time." I'm all for the direct approach, but when it comes to information gathering, subtlety usually works better. "Plus, if David goes over there and Cesar finds out, he's going to be furious. Charge you with interfering."

"Cesar?" Naomi slid a cookie on a plate in front of her brother.

David inhaled deeply. "The homicide detective, Cesar Garza."

"You call him Cesar?" She set a cookie before me.

I held up my palm. "No, thanks."

She took the plate for herself, her gaze never leaving my face. So much for avoiding the question.

"Yeah. I've known Cesar since we were kids." Way easier to explain than to get into the whole bisexual discussion over cookies with David. I leaned forward. "He'd kill me for meddling, too, so this will just have to be our secret."

"Let's go," David rose.

Naomi gave her brother a withering look with another cookie on the side. "Not you. Alma and I will handle this one."

Naomi sprung for an Uber. On the way, I asked her about rabbinical school and we discussed our favorite classes on the Bible.

"I lead services twice a month, teach, do Bar and Bat Mitzvah tutoring, and spearhead the social justice programs at Tikkun Olam. I only started last month, but so far I like it."

I told her about St. Giles' visiting shut-ins, housing a shelter in our parish hall one week a month, and the healthcare for the homeless task force I'd organized at the hospital. We swapped stories about wacky members of our congregations and exchanged laughs over preaching foibles while our driver frowned at us in the rearview mirror. The inside jokes only priests and rabbis can understand—further evidence we were perfectly suited for each other.

"How do you like St. Giles?"

"Love it. The bishop appointed me priest-in-charge to revitalize the parish. They're working hard, and growing, and they're great people. Plus, they feed me and bring me little gifts all the time. It's like having a dozen doting grandmothers. I have more flowery smelling hand soap than a queer girl can use in her entire lifetime."

"Soap's nice, but I like the food." She patted her trim tummy, sighed, and rested her head on my shoulder. "Best job in the world, right?"

"Absolute best." I closed my eyes and held still, hoping she wouldn't move.

The offices of Kearney Properties occupied the ground floor of a Nob Hill apartment building. Odd place for a real estate office, considering Kearney was so interested in eking every penny of profit from a property. One of those fifty-bucks-a-workout barre studios would net way more money there than his cubicle farm, which could be housed anywhere in the city more cheaply.

We entered. Right away, I recognized the meeting room to the left as the place where Kearney had given his wrong-sort-of-people press conference. One day, new tenants would need to smudge it with sage to ritually cleanse the evil.

I marched right up to the front desk. "Hi, my name is Allison Lemmon. I'm a master mixologist. Did you see the spread about me in Frisco Magazine?" Such an awful name for a magazine. Locals never call our fair city Frisco.

A young man with a bowtie and immaculately groomed handlebar mustache popped up from his swivel chair, which rolled backward. "Totally! Ms. Lemmon, I'm a huge fan. How can I help you?"

If you're feeling bad for the real Allison Lemmon, don't bother, I made her up.

"Well, I saw on the news about that horrible murder on Fourteenth Street, and I thought it would make a perfect location for the new high-concept cocktail bar I've just had financed. Is the property available now?"

"Well, technically, no. It's under lease. But..." He lowered his voice to a reedy whisper, yet it remained just as loud. "Between you and me, the new tenant might fall through."

At my side, Naomi stiffened and made a squeak in the back of her throat.

"Excellent," I said. "It must be kismet that someone killed that poor woman just when I needed a hot piece of real estate."

The receptionist blinked, likely flabbergasted silent by Allison Lemmon's self-absorption. I probably should have toned it down, made my character less memorable. But it's best not to second guess your instincts in improv scenes, and she seemed like the sort of heartless person Kevin Kearney might admire.

"When can we see it?" Naomi asked.

"Well, technically, it's an active crime scene."

"Well, technically, I need to sign papers by the end of the day, or else I'm going to locate my cocktail bar at 18th and Guerrero. Prime spot in the gourmet ghetto."

"It's a great property. Right between two three-star restaurants, where you can grab a drink while you wait for a table at either place. I think Allison should stick with it." Naomi emitted a wistful sigh and grinned.

Mr. Mustache focused on her. He was totally queer, but even he wasn't immune to her smile, which drew a blush to his cheeks.

He cleared his throat. "Let me see what I can do." He picked up the handset on a black desktop phone, which I only noticed because next to it stood a pristine white phone. Maybe he had direct lines to heaven and hell.

If so, we were getting the downstairs connection. "Hey, Tony. I've got a prospective tenant here for the Fourteenth Street property… Yeah, that one… I know. But if it's empty at the moment, you could sneak them in the back. Just stay behind the yellow tape."

Naomi glanced at me, her eyes widening.

An electric thrill bolted through me. This was far more than just the scoop on the keys we'd hoped for, including confirmation Kearney Properties considered itself above the law.

"Good. I'll meet you out front with them in two minutes." He smiled obligingly at us. "Just give me a minute to locate the keys to the property."

As soon as he was out of earshot, Naomi turned to me, one eyebrow up. "Allison Lemmon, renowned mixologist?"

I shrugged, secretly basking in her astonishment.

"What happens when Tony drives us away and Mr. Bowtie Googles your Ms. Lemmon?"

"Actually, his name is Mr. Mustache. And I don't know yet. I haven't gotten that far." I curled my fingers, trying to cling to her warm wonder instead of her harsh pragmatism. "But I know if we'd invoked David's name, we'd never have come this close."

Naomi sighed. "I seriously hope Tony doesn't trade in concrete shoes."

Mr. Bowtie Q. Mustache, esquire, hooked his head around the doorframe. "There's a slight problem with the keys."

"Oh?" Naomi cocked her head.

"The red-tagged master is missing."

Of course it was. But David's hadn't had a red tag. Did the set found at the crime scene?

Two things happened then. Heaven called on the white phone, and an ear-piercing honk sent me half an inch in the air. I turned toward its source and saw a shiny black town car at the curb.

The receptionist dashed back to his desk and grabbed the white handset. "Hello?"

Instantly, he yanked the phone several inches from his ear, conveniently permitting Naomi and I to hear the caller.

"—that woman! Bring her up here immediately."

Now Naomi swung her head toward me. "It seems someone upstairs is a fan of yours, Allison."

I took a deep breath. If the purple color rising from the man's bowtie up his neck was any indication, this might be the time to cut our losses.

"Thanks anyway." I spoke loud enough that he could hear me over the man shouting through the telephone. "But if you don't have a key, I suppose it's the gourmet ghetto for me." I locked my arm around Naomi's elbow and spun us.

Tony blocked the door. He looked exactly like you'd expect a concrete shoe salesman to look. I don't want to stereotype guys who resemble the cast of the Sopranos. I'm sure he's a perfectly nice man. Probably teaches Sunday school at St. Clare's. But he was thicker than me and Naomi put together, and he didn't happen to be stepping aside to wish us godspeed.

"Excuse me, Ms. Lemmon, if that is your real name, Mr. Kearney would like to meet you."

"Fabulous. Perhaps you can mix him up one of your specialties," Naomi chirped. "Maybe he'd like that one you call Deep Trouble?"

Damn—I liked this girl. I glanced at my watch. 4:45 p.m. "Why not? It's five o'clock somewhere."

Bowtie—yes, I now considered us on a first name basis—led Naomi and me into the lobby, pushing the up button on the elevator.

When the doors whooshed open, Tony stepped in behind us. He smelled like the too-piney aftershave Cesar's dad wore, which did not put me at ease. Mr. Garza wasn't my biggest fan.

Our escort pushed the button for the fiftieth floor.

"It'll be five o'clock here by the time we reach the penthouse," Naomi muttered.

In fact, it only took three minutes to zoom up to the top floor. When the elevator opened again, a small woman wearing a white pantsuit with a Nehru jacket greeted us, her silver hair pulled into a tight bun.

"Thank you, Tony. Mr. Kearney is waiting for his guests." She dismissed the brawny man with the lift of her chin. Either they didn't think we were a physical threat, or she was a white-clothed, old-lady ninja. Option B was totally awesome even though I preferred to think we weren't being forcibly detained.

That's when I noticed everything in the penthouse was white. There weren't even chrome fixtures on the doors or silver veins in the marble floor. Not a gray throw pillow in sight. Every surface was pure, clouds-of-heaven white.

Okay. So Kevin Kearney was more eccentric than I'd realized.

"Mr. Kearney asks all his guests to put these on over their shoes." The majorettedomo held up white surgical booties. I slid them over the soles of my boots. Naomi did the same with her Mary Janes.

"This way, please."

The penthouse was blindingly bright, with wall-to-wall windows. Kearney sat at a white table. When I'd seen him on the news clip, he'd been wearing a navy-blue sport coat and red tie. Today, he'd buttoned a white oxford up to the middle of his chest so that his faded orange chest hair sprouted from the top. An unidentifiable white food lay on his plate—yolk-less omelet? Tofu patty?

I had the crazy urge to find a pepper shaker and grind it all over his table and his shirt, too.

He did not stand as we approached. "What the hell are you doing here, Lee?"

"Um…" I know I'd eschewed the direct approach earlier, but now it was my only option. "Just wondering if you were the one who murdered my friend."

He laughed, a low, slow chuckle that sent invisible bugs crawling down my spine.

"The police already have their man."

Naomi sucked in a breath.

He squinted at her. "Who are you?"

"She's a friend." I inched closer to her. "Were you at the The Carlos Club late Wednesday night?"

"It's not The Carlos Club anymore. It's 800 14th St."

"And you wanted it back so bad, you knocked Cindy over the head to make sure you got your bar vacated on schedule?"

"Look, I'm glad that bitch is dead. But I didn't kill her."

Cindy's favorite T-shirt had read, *You say bitch like it's a bad thing.* Still, I didn't like the word in his mouth, a man so hateful he insulted the dead.

"You make a very convincing argument," Naomi said.

"I don't have to make an argument, I have an airtight alibi."

No doubt provided by Tony and the majorettedomo.

"What is it then? Where were you on Wednesday night?"

"That's between me and the police." He grinned.

Even though his teeth were straight and clean, there was something large and unpleasant about them. Perhaps they were veneers that didn't quite fit the size of his mouth. They were certainly too white.

"In fact, speaking of the police, I'm sure that polite Detective Garza would like to know you two are here snooping around."

I held my ground and tossed out a gambit. "How did your master keys end up at the crime scene?"

His blue eyes widened almost imperceptibly. He hadn't expected me to know that. "As I already told the police, I have no idea how that happened."

How interesting.

"And now, Tony will show you out."

He did so without mention of concrete shoes, and we breathed a sigh of relief in unison when we stepped safely onto the sidewalk outside Kearney's building.

We headed home more frugally, walking down the steep Nob Hill to catch BART in Union Square. On the train, Naomi invited me out for a drink.

Damn, I wanted to say yes, but I'd learned a hard lesson about late Saturday nights. Even raging extrovert priests get worn out on Sunday morning. Showing up irritable and just hung-over enough to find the smell of communion wine nauseating did not make me feel good about how I was living up to my ordination vows.

At home alone, I indulged in self-pity over how my career cramped my social life and tinkered with my sermon until I began to doze at my computer, then went to bed.

Chapter Seven

With St. Giles' gorgeous green silk vestments on, I entered the church and found it packed, with people standing in the side aisles. It wasn't even like this on Easter morning.

I'm not a crier—my emotions helpfully block my airways rather than exit my tear ducts—but all those visitors were there for Cindy. Their presence was enough to make my eyes prick with tears.

Before I came to serve as the vicar of St. Giles', Sunday attendance had trickled down to about two dozen people. They'd consolidated their services to a single, 9:00 a.m. Holy Eucharist. Over the last two years, we'd risen to eighty most weeks, and the small sanctuary grew cozy on well-attended days.

Prevailing wisdom said it was time to split into two services again, to leave room in the pews for newcomers. But the tight crowds exuded joy and togetherness in a way empty seats never could. So I'd ignored the sages of church growth and followed a restaurant management philosophy. If it's crowded, they will come.

If even a sliver of Cindy's mourners came back regularly, we'd have to start taking reservations on the Open Table app or return to the 8:30 and 10 a.m. schedule.

I turned on my lavaliere mic. "Blessed be God, Parent, Child, Holy Spirit."

"And blessed be their kingdom, now and forever," came the response.

Did you hear that, folks? At St. Giles', we know God's queerer than anybody in our queer city, refusing to be categorized, boxed in as one gender, so that all people, regardless of their plumbing and how they identify, know they're made in God's image.

Too bad half the people in the room weren't regulars, and their response was tepid at best.

"Newcomers and friends, let's try that again." I reminded them of their line, then bid the opening sentence a second time.

The reply was a roar, as if everyone present understood what the words meant about them and our sister Cindy.

I processed down the aisle as we sang "In Christ there is no East or West."

Too full of emotion, I tried not to look at any one person's face for moral support. If I made eye contact, I might have burst. I didn't even peek when a shimmer of mahogany waves made me wonder if Naomi was in the congregation.

The service proceeded slowly because I added in lots of guidance for the first timers in the pews. Still, it had the same joyful exuberance of every Sunday, and it buoyed me right until the moment I slipped into the pulpit. Only my senior warden Al seemed preoccupied. He wore his perpetually worried expression and, as usual, he scribbled on the margins of the bulletin nonstop throughout the entire liturgy.

I began with a passage from Jesus's sermon on the mount.

"You have heard what was said to people who lived long ago. They were told, 'Do not commit murder. Anyone who murders will be judged for it.' But here is what I tell you. Do not be angry with a brother or sister. Anyone who is angry with them will be judged."

Then I told the story of arguing with Cindy Wednesday night, in a way that flattered her, of course. These were her mourners, after all, and Lynn was right there in the front row. Plus, I'd learned from my preaching professor to tell stories that revealed my flaws, not ones that showed me as a victim or a hero.

"Jesus warns us that holding on to our anger, fanning its flames, leads us down a path toward violence. Instead, we should resolve our differences right away. We may not get another chance in this life to make peace with our brothers and sisters."

"Of course, sometimes our anger isn't about a personal slight, but a righteous cause. Stoking that fire fuels our passion for justice. But as every great change-maker has taught us, all the way back to Jesus and the Buddha, before we act, we must move past the anger and towards strategy, drawing on what we know is right to resist peacefully."

And lastly, I said the same prayer for Cindy that I had when I'd found her body. "Now, she is one of those saints in the light. And I trust she's still with us in a new way. I've heard her voice, ribbing me the way she always did. The good news is, in some mysterious way, Cindy and I have made peace after all. Because—and this is why we come together here every Sunday—love is stronger than death."

I scanned the faces in the pews. Some of the women had been at The Carlos Club on Wednesday night. Some of them had applauded me when I turned off "Everybody Dance Now" and again when I stood on the bar top and gave an empty inspirational speech.

No one clapped now. Instead, the church fell into a deep, reverent silence. I breathed it in, let it comfort me, convince me of my own words.

I'm sorry, Cindy.

Right back atcha, Alls.

Another deep breath, and I rose to continue the service. Next came the creed, the prayers, and the collection of an offering that overflowed the plates, dedicated to the GLBTQ Youth Center on Market Street. Then I stood behind the altar with my arms spread wide to begin the Eucharistic Prayer.

I sniffed. What was that smell? Onions.

I glanced around. Jenny Wong, who was serving as a Eucharistic minister, shrugged. I eyed the pita bread on the paten. It had telltale brown flecks of onion in it. Yikes. Clearly one of the altar guild ladies had bought the wrong package. Probably Lois, whose eyesight seemed to be failing fast. Mental note—I needed to check that she had enough help at home.

I glanced back at the sacristy. Were some of those cardboard-like communion wafers hiding somewhere? Oh, who cared?

"Well, folks—this is a little strange. Today, the body of Christ is onion flavored. I guess we're doing things differently in honor of Cindy."

A few chuckles rumbled in the congregation. They built up to a round of laughter, which caught hold of me, too, so that I stood, giggling, my arms still wide in the gesture of prayer.

There—two-thirds of the way back in the packed church—I glimpsed Naomi. Her gorgeous mouth was spread into a grin that seemed to be just for me.

Warmth rained on me as if from above. She'd come. Maybe I could listen to her give the sermon at next week's Shabbat services.

"The Lord be with you." I began the prayer, brimming with the peace and sense of profundity the service had brought. There, behind the altar, I'd never felt more grateful to be a priest, more certain of the calling that had gripped me the first time I'd walked in to Grace Cathedral as a teenager. God wanted me to be right here.

As soon as the service ended, I hung up my vestments and raced to the parish hall in search of Naomi. Where had she gone?

I spotted Lois of the bad eyesight instead. She returned a muffin to a plate and rushed toward me. "Reverend Alma, I am so sorry about the bread this morning. They must have changed the packaging. I always buy the one with the orange label."

"It's okay. I think we needed to laugh today. And it was perfectly delicious."

She giggled. "You are so refreshing, dear."

Would she still think so after I called her daughter about my concerns she needed more help? "I'd like to come visit you this week."

"Wonderful." She squeezed my hand in her bony one. "I'll make those vegan brownies you love."

"You are a saint."

Please, God, let her tell the salt from the sugar.

Behind her, people circled me at a distance, as if they all wanted a moment with the priest but didn't want to be pushy about it. Where was Naomi, and why wasn't the one person I wanted to see in my orbit?

Al smiled at me from near the coffee urn and headed my way. Great—this was so not the time I wanted to have our much-needed face-to-face. Would he whip out the laundry list of my leadership failures he'd been writing on the bulletin?

Before he reached me, Lynn pushed through the dense asteroid belt of parishioners. Her nose was head-reindeer red and raw around the nostrils. Ouch.

"Oh, Alma, that sermon…" She opened her arms, and I stepped close, accepting her hug. "It hit me right in the gut. Cindy and I were having so many problems. She must have told you?"

I wriggled free. "She told me a little." But I'd always suspected it was nothing close to the whole story, and I respected Cindy's impulse to keep marital strife private.

"It seems so stupid now." Lynn's lower lip trembled. "I'd forgive anything to have her back, you know?"

"I do."

She swallowed the tremulous lip, nodding, and grabbed my arm. "There's something I need to tell you—"

"Can you hear me?" A too-loud voice came over the parish hall sound system. Jenny, up on the stage.

What the heck was she doing?

"It's wonderful to see you all here. What a tribute to Cindy. On behalf of all her friends in this church, I sincerely thank you for being here. And I want to draw your attention to an issue that was near and dear to her heart—affordable housing. I campaigned with a promise to bring more low-income units onto the rental market, and you voted for me for the same reason."

I scanned the crowd for signs everyone found this impromptu speech as inappropriate as I did. On the contrary, all my satellites seemed positively rapt. Great—they were free to orbit Jenny for as long as they wanted.

She extended her hand, palms up, and indicated everyone in the room. "I want to invite you to a rally later this afternoon in China Basin. There's a property under development there with the potential for two hundred units. The Board of Supervisors needs to know you demand the developer designates twenty percent for affordable housing!"

The parish hall erupted in cheers. For all I found Jenny's presumption annoying, I had to grant her that, one—St. Giles' had been her church far longer than it had been mine, and two—affordable housing was one of the most important issues the city faced. Gentrification and rising rents contributed to Cindy losing her bar and possibly to her murder.

So why did I feel like Jenny was hijacking Cindy's death to increase turnout at her rally? That's how politics works.

"And lastly, I want to thank Alma Lee for her devotion not only to St. Giles', but to the whole Mission neighborhood, and my district—number nine! Alma, you are an inspiration to us all."

Sometimes being a priest means graciously accepting praise even when you feel cranky and jaded. I smiled and waved like I was in a parade—elbow, elbow. Wrist, wrist.

Where had Naomi gotten off to? Surely she would understand how I felt about Jenny's speech. I hung around coffee hour far longer than usual, munching on vegan pastries and wishing she would appear even though I knew it was unlikely. Then I helped the volunteers clean up.

Hazel Cummings always got confused about what went in the compost, the recycling, and the garbage so I gave her yet another demonstration.

Then I headed back to my house and texted Naomi. *Nice to see you this morning. Sorry I didn't get to say hi.*

I curled up in my bed and tried to slip into my traditional clerical Sunday afternoon nap with my phone in my hands. Every time I closed my eyes, I saw Cindy's gray face, the blood staining her hair brown. I remembered Kevin Kearney saying, "I'm glad that bitch is dead," and David yelling, "I put everything into my plans for this place."

Eyes dry and sticky, I stared at the wall and hummed "In Christ There is No East and West" to keep the memories from my mind. I must have fallen asleep eventually because I woke up when my alarm went off at four. A check of the screen confirmed what I already knew—Naomi had not replied to my text.

Chapter Eight

Alone in my tiny house, without a word from my crush, I shivered. Another cold June day, and my single wall-mounted gas heater wasn't up to the task. I peeked through the blinds and saw the fog blowing past. Time to gird myself.

I laced up my boots and zipped myself into my down jacket. Jenny's affordable housing rally was beginning ten blocks away. Any other night, I'd have put on my collar and made an appearance, even if I thought her announcement was impressively insensitive. But I observe a sacrosanct ritual every Sunday after my nap.

Hazel had sent me home with the leftovers from coffee-hour. I tossed them in my tote bag and headed for Lee's Grocery.

My parents still lived upstairs in the flat I'd grown up in. They'd inherited the store when my grandpa had been murdered for the contents of his cash register.

Sometimes I dreamed of finding him there, crumpled in a heap with a black hole in his forehead. My mouth had fallen open in a scream, and then Cesar's arms had come around me squeezing me so tight I couldn't fall apart. For weeks he'd been following me home from school, all gangly and determined, trying to win my attention. That day he'd earned my love.

Yeye had been old, he'd made tasteless jokes about being ready for his own death, but I'd believed he would live to be a hundred. I still missed his wheezing laugh, his wry sense of humor that neither my father nor me could ever translate into a language my mother understood.

The way Dad handled his grief was to gut the store and make

the changes Grandpa had refused. My father had seen how the neighborhood was changing, the gourmet ghetto springing up on 18th St. The Rainbow Grocery over on Division. The rising rents. His customers wouldn't be able to afford to live there much longer, and if he wanted to stay he would need to change with the times. He'd stocked organic produce, natural foods, local artisan cheeses and pantry products.

I'd learned the word gentrification by then, and we argued about pricing out the poorest neighbors, Yeye's cronies who'd been shopping there forever. With me and mom both at him, Dad agreed. He grandfathered in the regulars with a friends-and-family discount, which meant they were eating better, too. One woman who had played mahjong with my grandmother said switching to organic produce had cured her eczema.

When dad remodeled, he tore out the cash register stand in the center of the store where I'd found Yeye and put in an aisle along the side wall. Now I only saw the old counter in my dreams.

When I arrived, Dad was behind the new checkout stand. Mom spritzed greens in the produce section. I kissed them both on the cheek. Sometimes on Sunday evenings the store was busy with people doing their last-minute shopping for the week, but on that night it was mostly empty—hopefully everyone was at Jenny's rally.

Mom and I came to stand near Dad where we could chat.

"All right?" He didn't have to mention the murder for me to know what he meant.

"Church helped this morning. Lots of Cindy's friends came…"

"But?" Mom raised her brows, which she penciled in because she'd over-plucked in her youth.

But I keep seeing Cindy's dead body when I close my eyes.

But I lost a friend and Lynn lost her wife, and I'm worried the murderer is my latest crush's brother.

But Alma Lee doesn't get hysterical.

I gulped down the lump in my throat. "No buts. I'm carrying on. Cesar's on the case. I'm sure he'll solve it soon."

Both my parents smiled at the mention of his name. I never told them the gory details of how we'd hurt each other in our last months together. They welcomed anyone I introduced them to, but they'd always loved Cesar best, so I'd spared them.

"Are we still on for dinner a week from Friday?" Mom had

made reservations at Dad's favorite Thai restaurant for his birthday.

"Can't wait." And I'd have to find some time to shop for a gift.

"Let me get your bags." Mom disappeared into the storeroom.

I turned to Dad, who was watching me with a funny look. "What?"

"You seem tired."

Ridiculous. "I never get tired. I'm inexhaustible."

"I know. That's what worries me." He chucked me under my chin. "Take care of yourself."

Mom returned with two Lee's grocery reusable totes. I set the bags she gave me last week on the check stand and accepted the new ones. Like all the stores in the city, they gave their expired products to the Food Bank, but some perishables had too short a shelf life to bother.

Once I hefted up the heavy bags, she squeezed my neck again. I'm not the kind of person people fuss and fret over, not even my parents. Clearly, they were sensing my unease.

At the Sixteenth and Mission BART Plaza, I set the groceries next to the wall near Tom and Linda. They lived in a van they parked around the corner and sold her handmade jewelry. She'd spread her beaded necklaces out on a scrap of velvet.

Skinny Tom had a sweet tooth, so I handed him the bag of coffee-hour cookies and muffins.

"Thanks, Madré."

The regulars appeared, accepting bruised apples, browning bananas, wilted chard, and slightly limp broccoli.

Everyone had hugs and high-fives for me. I passed out pints of organic milk to the children in the plaza. The milk was still fresh although its use-by date approached. They guzzled them down right away. A little boy named Pedro blew me a kiss.

When the groceries ran out, I descended the stairs into the BART station with heavy feet. Distributing the food energized me, but more like a Red Bull than a good night's sleep.

The platform smelled like a porta potty, which called to mind Kevin Kearney's pristine penthouse. He'd probably have a panic attack over riding public transportation.

The train arrived at the Powell Street Station, and I ascended. Minutes later, I reached the Perfect Sip. A shiny black muscle car had pulled over to the curb. A glimpse of platinum hair facing away from the windshield suggested that my friend Suze was making out with the driver, her rock star husband Rush Perez.

The passenger door opened, and Suze exited the car.

"Boys aren't allowed," I shouted.

"I think you made that rule so you could have the girls all to yourself," Rush called back.

"Maybe." I winked.

Suze slammed the door. He shook his head and hit the gas as her musical laugh rang out on the sidewalk.

She grabbed my elbow and marched me into the bar. "I'm so sorry about what happened at The Carlos Club."

I squeezed her arm, drawing us closer. "Thanks."

"You knew the victim, didn't you?"

"Since high school. I went to her wedding."

In reply, Suze held my arm tight and led me to a table.

Lily arrived soon, and I found myself in a rare, quiet mood. They gossiped about the diocese, the clergy we knew, the latest escapades of our friend Jordan's uptight husband and their beautiful little girl Katharine Beatrice, my goddaughter.

Normally I rubbed my godmother status in Suze and Lily's faces every chance I got, but not that night. I only listened, glad to be with people who didn't mind my silence, who would never ignore a text message like Naomi had, who'd never argue with me, then get themselves murdered on my doorstep.

Although, I could hardly blame Cindy for that part.

The image of her lying there dead had cemented itself in the front of my mind. Would I dream of it always, like I did Yeye's corpse.

"Alma!"

I jerked my head up and found both my friends staring at me. "What?"

Lily winced. "I said your name three times."

"Sorry. I'm off in my own world."

"I'm worried about you." Suze reached for my hand and gave me a squeeze. She'd had her nails painted white, and she wore a bright white blouse that showed a drop of red wine on the sleeve.

And suddenly I understood about Kearney—he couldn't have killed Cindy. He probably couldn't even leave his apartment.

I grabbed my phone and sent Naomi a text. *With Kearney's crazy OCD, I don't think he ever leaves that building.* Even the press conference where I'd seen him on video had taken place in the ground floor offices.

Naomi replied to this text right away. *Dammit. That must be his alibi.*

"Who's Kearney?" Lily asked.

"And who's Naomi?" Suze leaned forward, her eyes bright.

The second question was too complicated to answer, so I took the first one.

"Kearney is the landlord of The Carlos Club. Remember how he and Cindy got into a nasty public battle, complete with name calling?"

Both my friends nodded.

"Well, he's one of the few people with a motive, so I snooped at his office, and he called me up to his freaky, germaphobe penthouse—"

"Wait." Lily flattened her palm onto her forehead. "You went to talk to a murder suspect?"

Technically, I'd gone in search of a set of keys, but, "Yeah."

Suze wagged her head. "Oh, no. No. No. No."

"What?" I crossed my arms.

"I think she means, you're not a detective." Lily cast Suze a sidelong look, then took a sip of wine.

"I know that. I'm just pastorally nosy."

"And you also know you aren't a professional matchmaker, a sex therapist, a union organizer, a public policy wonk, a nutritionist, or any of the dozen other pastimes you engage in on top of your incredibly demanding, more-than-full-time church job?"

My face heated. "I have a lot of passions."

"Uh huh." Suze guzzled her wine and poured herself more without offering Lily or me any.

The heat traveled down my neck. She was treading dangerously close to the barely scabbed over wounds Cesar had dealt me last year.

I refilled my glass. "There's a long tradition of clergy who solve murders."

"Name one."

"Brother Cadfael. Father Brown. Sydney Chambers. Clare Fergusson."

Lily cleared her throat. "You realize those are all characters in books?"

"So? Books are true." When they didn't immediately agree, I tacked on, "In the deepest sense of the word."

Suze burst out laughing. "Oh, my God. One day, Alma, you will realize you can't be everything."

I stood up fast, knocking my chair over. "I've got to go."

Lily reached for my wrist. "Wait. Don't leave. Suze doesn't mean it like that." She shot a sharp glare at our friend.

"Oh, I think she means it exactly like that."

My phone buzzed with a text. I glanced at the screen. Naomi had written again. *If it's not Kearney, David is still the prime suspect.*

I put the phone away. Suze and Lily both watched me, Suze's lips pursed. Lily elbowed her.

"Sorry," she muttered.

"She's just worried about you," Lily said. "We both are."

Suze sniffed. "When I saw 'Murder at St. Giles' in the Chronicle Friday morning, my heart stopped for a full minute, until I read that you were okay."

I nodded, my defenses softening, if not quite lowering completely.

"Please be careful," Lily said.

"And leave the investigating to the police," Suze added.

I nodded again.

My friends looked at each other, and Suze tilted her head. "She's completely ignoring us."

"Yep." Lily drained her glass of water. "As usual."

If anything good had come out of wine night, it was displacing images of dead bodies with memories of why the man I'd loved had left me again, for the final time, thirteen months ago.

It wasn't my friends' fault they were giving my wounds a salt scrub. I'd only offered them the superficial explanation—we wanted different things—which was and is completely true. Lily had just gotten back together with Eric, Rush had moved into Suze's life, and I didn't want to be a bummer. So I meddled in their lives, played the matchmaker, and acted generally blasé until my heart stopped aching.

My circulatory organ remained pain-free, but Cesar's criticism was a paper cut across all my fingertips that refused to heal.

"You have to decide, Alma. You can't be everything. I don't

want a wife who hangs out at the dyke bar, who never spends a night at home because of her causes, who puts her work before me every single time. I'm pretty sure that's even in the Bible—you can't be all things to all people. And I can't live off the crumbs of your attention."

Then he'd walked out of my house without letting me argue people often misquoted that passage from Paul. The great missionary had indeed become all things to all people, crossing cultural divides to spread God's love.

The satisfaction of being right about a Bible passage faded quickly when I realized Cesar wasn't coming back. I had to consider the rest of his complaint—that I put work before him and left him the scraps of my time. In thirteen months, I hadn't stopped loving him, but I had accepted our inherent incompatibility. We weren't right for each other. While Naomi... She would understand my work, and I would do the same for her.

A year and month absent from my life, then suddenly Cesar showed up at the murder scene and punched me to stop my crying, which proved he still loved me, too. But love does not make people compatible. That's just a fact of life.

Any news? I texted him from the depths of the BART station.

When I was commuting to seminary on the train, they hadn't had cell coverage in the tunnel. To me, it qualified as a Biblical miracle that my phone worked underground.

Water into wine. Cell signal beneath the city.

His reply came fast. *You tell me. Did you catch Kearney red handed?*

Shit. See what I mean? Love and happiness—not the same thing. I called him, just to make sure he would not arrest me for criminal meddling, or whatever label the penal code applied to my activities.

Hah. Penal code. That would have made him laugh.

The phone rang.

Did Naomi laugh at stupid dick jokes? A remarkable number of lesbians don't think they're funny, possibly because they aren't acquainted first hand with how spectacularly ridiculous a penis is. And I do mean that—both spectacular and ridiculous.

More ringing.

This part was always so hard for Cesar—that I could want him, that we burned up the sheets together, yet I never stopped wanting women just as much. Not that I cheated. I simply felt attraction beyond the moderate bi-curiosity he might have tolerated, and I had set metaphorical bed linens on fire with lots of women too, in our off-again phases.

It niggled at him, the fear he wasn't enough for me. And so he'd dumped me, leaving me with a parting gift—the accusation that I'd never be enough for anyone.

His voicemail picked up. "This is Cesar Garza. I can't take your call right now. Please leave a message. If you need to reach someone immediately… "He rattled off the number for the Mission Station dispatcher, then repeated it. The beep crackled.

"You wimp. I know you can take the call. You're just watching soccer with Mario."

He did not call back.

What if he wasn't with his brother? What if he was with a woman who devoted herself to him, stroked his ego, made him feel like a man because she had a singular focus—him. I hoped they would make each other very happy. Because I was happy being myself. Not merely being the one thing he wanted, but all the things I wanted to be.

Mission Street was quiet at 10:00 p.m. on Sunday. I kept my head up, alert. A signal not to mess with me. More than once, a john had followed me home, thinking he could pay me for a blowjob in some dark doorway. But they spooked easily when I politely informed them I wasn't a sex worker.

I reached the church, unlocked the gate, and slipped through the dark side yard toward my house. Something moved in the corner of my vision. I froze.

Was someone lurking back here?

Shit. I blew out a breath. Just a tree, blowing in the breeze. It probably rustled like that every night I passed by, but I'd never been so wound up, never truly felt afraid in my neighborhood. Now, even my earthquake-shelter of a vicarage didn't feel safe.

Would this fear fade once the police caught Cindy's murderer, or would I startle whenever the wind rustled a tree?

Chapter Nine

Tish, Lois and Hazel attended Morning Prayer the next day. Jenny must have pulled a late night at her rally, and who knew where Al was. Curating his collection of heavily critiqued Sunday bulletins, so they were ready to present to me?

Light shone through St. Giles' stained glass, dappling the area where we sat reciting psalms, canticles, and enjoying stretches of silence. The quiet service calmed my jittery nerves so I felt almost ready for the day.

Afterward, Hazel pressed a vegan blueberry muffin into my hand. She knew my tendency to run late, then dive into work, accidentally skipping breakfast. The divine aroma of toasted oats escaped the brown bag. Well cared for, and soon to be well fed, I truly could tackle a day's work.

"Thank you." I clutched the muffin to my heart.

Kayla had arrived early and opened the office. She stood, hunched over my desk. Panic grabbed my neck in a chokehold. She'd been threatening to clean in there and impose an organizational system on my papers. I'd employed every excuse and distraction in my quiver. I was nearly out of arrows.

"Good morning." I chirped with false cheer, scanning the front office for something—anything—to draw her away from the desirable disorder of my desk. My gaze settled on a red and gold tin with a bow on it next to the kettle. "What's this red box?"

She appeared in my doorway. "It's for you."

I unfolded the gift tag. *For Mother Alma—Green tea with licorice, dandelion and chrysanthemum. For courage.*

Yeye used to drink a similar blend of herbs to support liver and gallbladder function, the organs that make you bold and brave in Traditional Chinese Medicine. And I was presently in need of some extra courage.

"Who's it from?"

"I don't know. It was there when I got here. I assumed someone gave it to you yesterday."

"Nope." People often gave me thoughtful tokens, hence my collection of flowery hand soap. They frequently gifted them anonymously, too, but I knew the giver because they left the items with Kayla.

"Someone with a key must have dropped it off," she said.

Mentally, I listed the possibilities. Al, Jenny, Tish, our treasurer, the current music director Pete, the former music director Paul, Stephen Shaw the previous senior warden… the list grew longer and longer.

Kayla dropped into her desk chair and moved her mouse to wake up her computer. "Between the money counters bringing in the plate collections and current and former members of the bishop's committee, half the parishioners have keys to this place."

"True." On Jenny's advice, I'd requested a change of locks on the cottage for that very reason. No need having helpful parishioners letting themselves in to check if my home was too drafty.

I filled the kettle and scooped some loose-leaf tea into my steeping ball. Its scent wafted up from the box, different from Yeye's brew—sweeter, with a hint of melon. My stomach growled, reminding me of the muffin waiting for me. I poured hot water over the tea, carried my mug and brown bag to my delightfully disarrayed desk and tucked into my breakfast along with the task topmost on my scattered papers, a second tardy notice from the diocese.

I'd failed to send in my continuing education hours form back in December, then ignored the reminder in March. The task hadn't merely shuffled itself to the bottom of the messy pile, although it was possible the second notice was still there somewhere. I'd simply stalled out on the form twice, unsure exactly what to count as continuing ed. The healthcare public policy course I'd done at the UC Berkeley Extension? The online Sex Therapy 101 class I'd taken after a particularly challenging premarital counseling session? The urban foraging workshop I'd completed? (Did you know a savvy gatherer can live off the edible mushrooms, leafy greens and wild onions that grow in Golden Gate Park? And I'm not talking about pillaging the arboretum's garden patch.)

I'd learned invaluable things in each, but I knew the bishop's staff expected a list like, "Preaching through Lent and Easter," and "How to organize your Sunday school rota."

I took a swig of the tea for courage, bittersweet with a hint of melon. Pen in hand, I filled out my form truthfully, listing all my continuing ed—Alma style—ignoring Suze's admonition in my head. *You aren't a professional matchmaker, a sex therapist, a union organizer, a public policy wonk, a nutritionist, or any of the dozen other pastimes you engage in on top of your demanding, more-than-full-time church job.*

My belly clenched. The tea was strong. I pinched off a bite of muffin and scarfed it down so I didn't drink my courage on an empty stomach. Scanning my desk, I searched for the next piece of paper that represented an interesting or urgent task. Sadly, I did not receive the spiritual gift of joyfully attending to the boring and important ones. Under a stack of budget spreadsheets Tish had asked me to review, my seminary's quarterly newsletter peeked out. In the spirit of collegiality and support of the institution, perusing it was surely one of my priestly duties.

I flipped open the newsletter and saw the smiling face of one of my male classmates. He was a total nincompoop the same age as me, with three blond children and a full-time-mom wife, and he'd landed the job of cathedral dean somewhere in the Midwest. They deemed him qualified because he looked like their ideal dean and his Norman-Rockwell-painting of a family evoked feelings of safety and nostalgia. Meanwhile, my bishop took pity on me when I couldn't find a job out of seminary and appointed me priest-in-charge of a floundering church. Not that I'd trade St. Giles' for any Midwestern cathedral that would hire for type instead of skill.

An intestinal grumble signaled that the patriarchy made me sick. Either that, or the tea wasn't agreeing with me. I broke off another bite of Hazel's muffin, but it suddenly smelled sulfurous, and it had the gritty texture of a crumbling sea sponge on my tongue. I gave my breakfast a break.

For the next half an hour, I answered email and did a round of pastoral care on social media, visiting the various outlets to reach the different generations of St. Giles' membership. I texted Lynn a heart emoji. *Thinking about you.*

She replied with the thank-you hands, which always looked like praying hands to me. Prayer and gratitude really are inseparable, so the similarity made sense, symbolically speaking.

My irritable stomach settled down, and I relaxed into my desk chair. I pulled a Biblical commentary off the shelf to scan what it said about next Sunday's lessons. The set had belonged to a former rector who'd left them in the office, and they were outdated compared to the modern, feminist volumes Suze and Lily used. But St. Giles' couldn't afford to buy me those, and I kind of enjoyed getting steamed up over the oppressive theology in the arcane set. It helped motivate me to preach compassion and justice.

Nausea swam up my throat all at once, leaving me only enough time to reach my trashcan next to my desk. The first wave hit me hard and fast, emptying the meager contents of my stomach in the plastic-lined bin.

As I shuddered, Kayla entered and crouched beside me. She tucked my hair behind my ear. I rested on my knees, waiting for the wave to pass. As soon as she took the trashcan to empty, the urge to vomit stole over me again. I dashed from my office, past her desk, reaching the toilet just in time to heave again, bringing up only bile. I guess my courage tea had stimulated my gall bladder.

"Too much wine at the Perfect Sip?" Kayla asked neutrally, handing me a damp paper towel.

"No. Not that. Maybe the tea, or Hazel's muffin?"

"Vegan baked-goods are not known for harboring food-borne illnesses. Considering the number of hands you shake, my money's on a stomach flu."

I grunted, admitting the possibility. "I think I'll just lay down right here."

Getting horizontal in the cramped restroom proved more difficult than I'd anticipated. My short body did not fold neatly into a space only as wide as the toilet and a tiny, wall-mounted corner sink. I bonked my head on the toilet paper dispenser, then the molding along the floor.

"How about lying down in your bed instead of turning yourself into a pretzel on this dubiously clean floor? We can hit your house with a rock if we open this window."

She had a point. Perks of living on-site. But at the moment, that stone's throw felt as long as the circumference of the earth. "Can't." I groaned into my armpit, where I'd buried my face.

"Come on, I'll walk with you."

By the time we'd reached my bed, it was more accurate to say she'd carried me than accompanied me. She tucked me in up to my chin and brought a whole stack of nested mixing bowls, "Just in case."

"Who can I call?" she asked.

"I'll be fine. Need to rest."

"Whatever you say. Drink this water slowly." She set a cup with one of my stainless steel reusable straws on my nightstand. "And don't come back today. If by some divine mercy I've escaped your germs so far, I don't want you to breathing the same air as me."

I drifted off to sleep before I heard her close my front door and woke when it slammed shut some time later.

"*Mija?*"

"*Aqui*, Mama." My mother was the only person I'd given my spare key.

She rushed into my bedroom and clucked over me, explaining that Kayla had called the grocery store. She took my temperature—slightly high—and fed me ginger tea, which I promptly threw up. I began to doze again and made her promise she wouldn't waste a day as my sick nurse. She left but first insisted she would return in the late afternoon. Again, I fell asleep before the door to my house banged closed.

The next time I woke, both my thoughts and my vision were clearer. The pain in my abdomen had eased. The house was silent, but a sensation skating over my skin told me I wasn't alone.

"Who's there?"

A dark figure, tall and lean, appeared in the door of my bedroom. Cesar.

"Who let you in?"

He dangled a key on a dragonfly chain from his fingers—my mom's copy.

"How are you feeling?" He crossed his arms and leaned against the doorframe. Once upon a time, he'd stood just like that, smiling at me as I lay on the bed like I was everything he could want. I'd fooled us both on that front, at least for a while.

"Better." I dug my elbows into the mattress and shimmied until I was more or less upright, leaning heavily against my pillows.

"I'm taking you to the hospital."

"Are you kidding? I'm fine. Just a little stomach bug."

"You're sure?"

"One hundred percent. What are you doing here?"

"Kayla called me."

"There's no need for that. My mom already came by. I don't also need Nurse Garza on duty."

"That's not why, Alls." He held up a zip-lock bag. Inside the clear plastic was a red and gold tin—the tea I'd brewed this morning. "She said you thought it hadn't agreed with you and suspected that someone gave it to you for that purpose."

Cesar and Kayla—two people who would never, ever resort to acupuncture and herbs over invasive Western medicine. "Don't be ridiculous. It's tea to promote liver and gallbladder health. Yeye drank the stuff all the time. It just didn't agree with me. I probably already have a very healthy liver and gallbladder. That's why I'm so bold."

Cesar snorted. "That's what it's supposed to be. But the lab will tell us what it really is. In the meantime, no eating food randomly given to you by strangers. Even better—stick with stuff sealed up in packages."

"No way." Aside from my microwave popcorn addiction, I tried to stay away from any and all shrink-wrapped foods. "Besides, why would anyone want to hurt me?"

He frowned at me, tucking his chin with astonishment. "Because they think you know something about Cindy's murder." He utterly failed to keep the *duh* from his voice.

"I know nothing."

"Believe me, I'm aware of that, but the killer could think Cindy crawled to St. Giles' to tell you who bashed her over the head. Or they got wind of your snooping at Kearney's place and think you're getting too close."

"How does making me sick for a day solve those problems?"

He shifted his weight to lean on the other side of the doorframe, lifting his brows and pressing his lips together.

Oh. Right. It didn't. I gulped, the sensation painful in my dry throat. "You think this was a murder attempt by poisoned tea?"

"It's not the craziest thing I've heard. Guilty people are desperate."

"It's the craziest thing I've ever heard. Kill the priest on the slim chance she knows something? No way." I shook my head, silently wondering if David Cohen was that desperate, or if Kearney was involved after all.

Cesar sat on the edge of my bed stiffly, like he was trying not to remember hitting snooze on his phone alarm to hold me a little longer in the mornings we'd woken here together.

He trained his eyes on his shoes. "Who knows you're a tea drinker?"

"Half the Mission. I always have a cup in my hand. And the baristas know my order by heart."

A strangled sigh squeezed its way out of his throat. "Think, Alma. Do you know something without realizing it?"

Beneath his frustration with me, I heard his worry for my safety. Silly, misplaced, but enough to melt my ribs and turn my heart squishy soft.

I shook my head. "I can't think of anything. And when the lab results come back from that tea, it will not show anything except a bunch of Chinese herbs that will make the technicians scratch their heads."

Cesar rolled his eyes. "All the lab techs and forensic pros are Chinese American. I bet all their *yeyes* drank liver tea too, and they'll be able to tell if this one is poisoned."

Fair point. Mama's cop shows, with their token minorities, didn't do justice to the glorious diversity of my fair city.

"Good." I shimmied back down into the bed, pulled the covers up to my chin, and closed my eyes. "I look forward to them proving me right."

He huffed, and the mattress shifted. A moment later, a soft thud sounded near my head, and I opened my eyes. He'd replaced my untouched glass of water with a fresh one.

"Thanks."

He put his big hand on the top of my head, like I did when I blessed an infant too young to take communion. "Don't die, Alls."

"Sure thing, baby," I murmured, already dozing off again.

When I woke again, it was dark outside and my mom sat in a chair by my bed watching something on her phone.

I reached for mine on the nightstands and saw I'd missed a message from Naomi.

There's something I need to tell you about David. I'm scared.

My heart stuttered. She was scared, and she'd reached out to me. Maybe her disappearing act at church didn't mean she wasn't interested.

Then chills ran up my arms. I wanted Cindy's murderer found, but I didn't want it to be her brother.

Can we meet somewhere?

I sat up and the room spun.

Mama jerked up from her chair. "*Mija*, don't move so fast. You need to eat something."

Coffee shop? Bar?

As much as I hated to admit it, Mama was right. I'd probably be fine by morning, if I could keep down some fluids and toast. But I was in no shape to meet Naomi at the moment.

The phone buzzed in my hands. *Your place?*

My hollow stomach sank. Wasn't that my luck?

I replied, my thumb-typing clumsy from lightheadedness. *Not tonight. Didn't feel well today, but on the mend. Can I buy you breakfast?*

Sure. Sounds great.

Would it be weird to invite her to breakfast at my place? Yes. It sounded like a sleazy pick-up line.

I have Morning Prayer at 8:30. Meet at St. Giles' at 9?

Her reply was a grinning emoji that had nothing on her gorgeous smile. *See you then.*

I submitted to my mother's ministrations and kept down a mug of ginger tea and an entire package of saltine crackers before falling asleep again, only to dream of the lovely Naomi in need of my help.

Chapter Ten

I felt like my normal self when I woke in the morning. Still, I obediently made sure to brew my tea at home, even though Cesar was totally paranoid to think I'd been poisoned.

The usual suspects attended Morning Prayer—Jenny Wong, Lois, Hazel, and Al. At the end of the psalm, Cesar strode in on his long legs. When would men's fashion go back to looser pants? His thighs were so damn distracting. Or maybe it was remembering his big palm on my head and his words, sweetly whispered, *Don't die, Alls.*

He sat in the pew nearest the door, and I studiously avoided looking in his direction and continued the service. The hospitable Hazel popped up and invited him to come up to the choir stalls where the five of us sat. He shook his head—big surprise.

Jenny caught my eye and raised her brows, tipping her head at Al. He would not want his Morning Prayer interrupted by a murder investigation.

I just smiled and kept on praying. Everybody had ideas about what I should want and how I should act. It usually worked remarkably well to just ignore them and do what I knew I was supposed to do. In this case, get through the service so I could enjoy an interfaith breakfast with the city's most charming rabbi.

We ended the service with the Prayer of St. Chrysostom, but I didn't rush to Cesar. I made plans to visit Lois at three, listened to Hazel's concern for her sick Jack Russell, invited Al to lunch. He seemed pleased although he wasn't free to meet until Thursday. Jenny gushed about the rally. Two hundred people had filled the vacant lot and the local T.V. stations had sent news vans.

"Congratulations. Maybe you'll get more units than you're asking for."

She steepled her fingers. "Bwah ha ha. Next I take over the world."

I laughed. "If only all evil geniuses cared about affordable housing."

She cast Cesar a glance. He still sat in the back pew, his phone screen illuminating his high cheekbones. "I suppose we shouldn't keep the hard-working detective waiting any longer."

"Probably not." I marched down the aisle and propped my hip against the pew. "Yes?"

Lazily, he lifted his eyes from his screen. "Lynn lied. She wasn't at work for several hours in the middle of her shift. We have her on camera going through the toll plaza on the bridge."

"What?" Something whispered in the back of my mind, but Cesar kept talking and it slipped away.

"Turns out, in the last two weeks, the Oakland police answered three calls for domestic disputes at their address. Twice they had to haul Cindy away and let her cool off in a cell."

"Oh my God. Did she hit Lynn?" Maybe the murder had been self-defense?

"No violence reported. Just angry screaming that disturbed the neighbors. The Oakland guys picked her up this morning. They're bringing her into the station. From what they said, she flipped out when they showed up. She's babbling, ranting, not making a lot of sense."

"Hell. Do you think she killed Cindy?"

"I've seen this reaction before in guilty people. Not every murderer is cool as a cucumber."

"Oh, God." I wanted it to be Lynn even less than David Cohen. Could she really have killed her wife? I remembered her smiling up at Cindy, both of them wearing white bridal gowns in a grassy field in Tilden Park. "Do you remember how happy they were at their wedding?"

"Yeah." He looked past me toward the altar. "I remember lots of formerly happy people. It has a way of not lasting."

From the bitter edge in his voice, I was nearly certain he'd been watching football with Mario last night and not enjoying the company of a perfect woman.

He stood up.

"You're leaving?"

He raised one broad shoulder. "It seemed like you should know, seeing as she's your friend."

"Thanks." I stepped aside, letting him exit the pew.

He stopped mere inches from me and pulled out his badge, shoving it in my face. "Now that you're no longer puking your guts out, it's my duty to remind you I'm the detective assigned to this case, and you are a meddlesome friend of the victim. If the chief got wind of you going to Kearney's on Sunday night, he'd arrest you instantly, and I'd be guilty by association."

"So don't tell him." I sounded surly, even to myself.

"I won't, but you can't assume Kearney will keep quiet."

"Well, they're hardly golf buddies. Kearney probably hasn't left that building since the turn of the century."

Cesar cocked his head. "Picked up on that, did you?"

"The surgical booties were a clue." I didn't want to admit it had taken me twenty-four hours to arrive at the hypothesis. Though, presumably Kearney had offered up the fact as an alibi to Cesar, no deduction required.

"Don't assume he's not well-connected. He throws swanky parties on his rooftop garden. A lot of people are in his pocket."

"And a very clean pocket it is, I'm sure."

Cesar laughed.

"Hey, did you follow up on Jenny Wong's tip about that reporter from *The City Weekly*?"

"Yeah. It didn't pan out. He's been in London since last Monday."

"Oh." I was strangely disappointed. If only the guilty party were a stranger who was in no way related to my current crush.

"Hello?" As if I'd summoned her, Naomi's voice rang out in the entry hall. "Alma?"

"In here." I glanced at my watch. 9:05 a.m. "That's my breakfast date." I shoved Cesar toward the door. "Nice of you to drop by." Then I paused. "Seriously. Thanks for letting me know about Lynn. And I will try not to do anything that could get you in trouble with the chief."

"Somehow, that isn't at all reassuring."

Naomi appeared in the doorway dressed for the office in slacks and a blouse. She looked from me to Cesar and back. "Is this a bad time?"

Cesar took her in, then gave me a long stare that made my cheeks heat. Damn. How could he know I was interested in her? It's not like 'pretty femme rabbi' was my established type. More likely Naomi was just objectively attractive.

"Nope. Not a bad time at all. I'm just leaving. You two have a nice breakfast."

Chapter Eleven

Breakfast is a hit-or-miss meal for vegans, but not in the Mission District. I led Naomi to my favorite cafe and ordered the chia pudding with caramelized bananas and a second cup of green tea. In a nod to Cesar's insistence I eat packaged food, I tore open my teabag myself.

Naomi looked at the menu a long time, flipping it over repeatedly.

"Nothing looks good?" I asked.

"Normally, I like eggs for breakfast."

"Try the tofu scramble," I suggested.

"I avoid tofu—all those stray estrogens." She patted her pelvis. "I'm not getting any younger, and I want to keep my reproductive chances good."

Okay. So she wanted to be a mom, like Lynn, like Cesar wanted to be a dad. Godmotherhood to baby Katie, who lived a just-right two hours away, suited me well. But Naomi's desires weren't a deal breaker. With the right woman when I was a little more...

I couldn't even finish the sentence in my mind. Responsible? Mature? Boring? Singularly focused? Things I had no interest in being.

When my stomach growled loudly, she settled on the coconut milk yogurt parfait with extra walnuts, and the waitress left us alone.

"So tell me what's got you scared?"

She glanced around the cafe and seemed to satisfy herself we were out of eavesdropping distance. Then she took a deep breath and began. "David's shoes are missing."

I leaned closer. "Go on."

"It's his favorite pair. They're Scamper wingtips with a sporty sole that my mom bought him for his birthday, because he didn't own shoes to wear to a nice restaurant."

This compared to Cesar, who had more pairs of shoes than me, to match his excessive number of pricey suits. I prefer ankle boots—combat, cowboy, kick-ass—any variety. When you're only five feet, they add to your gravitas as well as your height. Like my clothes, most of my shoes come from one of Mission Street's many thrift shops, full of designer cast-offs. Cesar did not enjoy that particular shopping venue. They never had suits to fit his tall, lean frame.

Naomi's parfait came. She poked at it warily with her spoon.

"Coconut milk is great for the brain." I scooped up a spoonful of quivering chia pudding, made with cashew nut milk.

"Oh, good. It's just as important as my uterus, after all."

I quite liked her brain, so I would argue it was even more so. With so many foster kids and orphans in the world, who needed a uterus?

I watched a mouthful of her parfait disappear between her full lips. Her red lipstick didn't smear, probably that stay-on-all-day kind. As she ate, her bracelet glinted in the light.

"Is now a good time to tell me about the *Song of Songs*?"

Her gaze fell to the text, and grief took hold of her face. Okay, so it was an aspirational quote. The winter wasn't past yet; the rains still lingered.

"It's okay. You don't have to—"

"I got dumped by my girlfriend. The day we graduated from college. We'd already packed my car to move together, so I could start rabbinical school. It was…" She blew out a big breath and squeezed her eyes shut. "Out of the blue I lost my best friend, the future I wanted… It was hard to get over." While wearing that piteous expression, her use of the past tense seemed a little dodgy, even after what must have been at least four years.

"You stopped talking to her?" In my experience, lesbians almost always stayed friends through breakups, unlike Garzas.

"She stopped talking to me. Said she needed a clean break to find herself again. I heard she's pregnant, so I guess she did, with someone else."

"Ouch."

"Yeah." She pulled a pained smile.

"Listen, I know we just met, but from where I'm sitting, your ex was an idiot to give you up."

"Thanks." Naomi's eyes sparkled with what might have been tears. "We were young. She did what was right for her." She gulped some of her steaming coffee, which she apparently preferred black, if dairy wasn't an option.

My ribs squeezed tight as her pain sank into me. I wanted this woman to feel happy, to feel loved. I was more than willing to sign up for the job.

"What about you? Any wrenching breakups in your ancient past?"

Now was not the time to explain that the man who suspected her brother of murder had broken my heart.

I shook my head. "Just the ordinary relationships running their course. I guess it's always about finding yourself, knowing what you really want and need, and what you can't give up, no matter how much you love someone."

Naomi frowned thoughtfully. Crap—I'd said too much. She cocked her head, clearly queuing up a probing question. Answering it would probably require obvious evasion or outright lying if I wanted to leave Cesar out of it.

Time to change the subject to the mystery at hand.

"So your brother's shoes are missing?" I blew over my steaming green tea. Not as good as the gunpowder variety I brewed at home, but decent enough.

She tugged at the ends of her hair. "The police sprayed the bottoms of every other pair in the house with luminal to check for blood."

My throat closed around a mouthful of pudding. It may as well have been a whole walnut in its shell.

"And if one pair is missing, maybe David tossed it to hide evidence?"

Naomi nodded, her luscious lower lip trembling.

"Did you ask him?"

"He said Melissa threw them away to spite him."

"But you don't believe him?"

"I'm nearly certain he wore them to The Carlos Club the night of the party, and she left the day before."

Well damn. He was lying to his own sister. Things were looking better for Lynn by the minute.

"Did you point that out to him?"

She shook her head, yanking her napkin from her lap to wipe her eyes, then dab at her nose. "I was too afraid of what he'd say. I can't stand to think of him doing something so violent."

Nodding, I took a sip of tea. Maybe if I abandoned my twenty questions routine, she would just tell me everything I needed to know to help, or at least comfort her.

"When we were in high school, he discovered this litter of kittens mewling up a storm under our shed two days after a cat was run over on our street. He hid them from my parents inside the shed and hand fed all five of them every morning and afternoon. He got kicked off the baseball team for missing practice to take care of his kittens. When Mom found them, she was sweet about it, but she told him he had to give some of them away. He absolutely refused. Slept in a tent outside next to the shed. The kittens would climb in his sleeping bag with him all night long."

Oh, geez. The guy who'd gone nose to nose with Cindy, fists curled, and was presumably cheating on his wife with that fashion wannabe, was an animal lover?

I blew out a breath. "Did she let him keep them?"

"Yep. He won. But then they grew up, and five cats in our suburban New Jersey neighborhood meant a songbird slaughter. Every time they brought a dead bird to our back door, it broke his heart like finding the kittens had in the first place. Plus, the neighbors got out their pitchforks and confronted Mom at the mailbox.

I pictured an older version of Naomi facing down an angry mob.

"So he got them all collars with bells. Either the birds were dumb, or the cats were super-stealthy hunters. Finally, he sewed extra bells around all the collars. Those damn cats were like a herd of reindeer, jingling through the neighborhood year-round."

"And the birds?"

"Never brought another one home. So, see, David couldn't have killed Cindy."

For someone who'd deduced my occupation from a few sparse clues, this seemed like a careless fallacy. People are often kinder to animals than they are to their fellow humans.

But it was probably best not to point that out. I wouldn't be reasonable if someone accused my parents of murder, or Suze,

Lily, and Jordan, who were the closest things I had to siblings. Plus, that image of teenaged David in a sleeping bag, playing mama cat to a litter of orphaned kittens was some poignant schmaltz.

"If he's such an animal lover, why doesn't he have a pet cat?" I scooped up a perfectly caramelized banana and it slid down my throat, for the moment free of walnut-sized emotions.

"Melissa's allergic. Not just to cats. To everything. David once brought home an iguana, and the damn thing had her sneezing like crazy."

"Seriously? That has to be psychosomatic."

"I looked it up. It's a real thing." Naomi took her first bite of her parfait. Mouth full, she said, "Damn, this is delicious."

Score!

We ate our breakfast in silence, and I pondered how to respond to her revelation about the shoes. Obviously, I would have to tell Cesar. Hopefully he could protect my identity as the source of the information.

I could hear him loud and clear in my mind. *Sure, Alls, wouldn't want to hurt your chances of getting laid.*

It would be better if I could convince her to tell him, so she didn't feel betrayed.

She scraped the bottom of her parfait glass clean and licked her spoon. "So, what we have to figure out is, if it's not David and it's not Kearney, who could have killed your friend?"

This was like a pastoral visit to someone who has stage four cancer and tells you how they will beat it with the power of prayer, positive thinking, and the powdered wings of a newly discovered Amazonian insect. I had to help Naomi face the facts.

"That, and where your brother's favorite shoes went."

Her shoulders slumped.

"I'm sorry." I reached across the table.

She took my hand and squeezed it. "Don't be sorry. I called you. I know he's hiding something, but I can't believe he's a murderer."

"My grandpa was murdered fifteen years ago."

"Oh, God. How awful."

I shoved aside the image of his body. "It was an armed robbery. Here in the Mission. The police found the murderer. He was just a kid. My age. When the trial was happening, I couldn't stop thinking about his parents. About how they must have felt, and how they wouldn't stop loving him, even though he'd done something so awful."

Naomi closed her eyes and pressed on her lids, then drew her fingers together to pinch the bridge of her nose.

"Like God." I squeezed her warm, soft hand.

Eyes closed, she pulled a sad smile. After a deep breath, she opened them. "All that's true. But still, I know he's innocent, and I will find a way to prove it. If you don't want to help me, I understand. You've already done so much."

"Hey, I'm in. I want justice for Cindy." And I knew what she meant about knowing someone was innocent. I could still see the smile on Lynn's face at her wedding when Cindy had leaned in to kiss her. No matter how crazy she was acting, she wasn't capable of bludgeoning her wife to death.

Cesar would shake his head woefully at my naivety and say everyone was capable of murder.

"So, what's next?" Naomi asked. "Can you use your connection to the detective to…"

I didn't hear the rest of her sentence. My mind had wandered to Lynn in one of those horrid interview rooms, a hot light glaring down on her, although I'm pretty sure they had fluorescent bulbs in the Valencia Street Station. Guilty or not, she was in quite a pickle, and the chances were she needed a priest.

"What is it?" Naomi asked.

"It's the victims wife. I think she might be having a pastoral emergency."

"Go." She waved me off. "Breakfast's on me."

Oh, Naomi. She understood perfectly. Could there be a more perfect woman?

Chapter Twelve

I dashed back to St. Giles' to grab my prayer book and stole in case she wanted to make a confession. Was there anything else I needed?

Confession. If Lynn told me she'd killed Cindy, could I really pronounce God's forgiveness on her?

I'd eventually forgiven that frightened, trembling teenager for killing Yeye, but it took longer than four days, and I was never called upon to be his priest.

I burst through the glass doors of Mission Street Station, breathing rapidly. Cesar glanced up from where he was chatting with a pretty woman staffing the front counter.

When he saw me, he rolled his eyes, then glanced at his watch. "Short breakfast. I thought I'd have you out of my hair for at least an hour."

I puffed. "I'd like to see Lynn." I gasped for another breath. "As her priest."

"Out of shape, aren't you?"

If I weren't in a police station wearing my clerical collar, I would absolutely have shot him a bird. I didn't run marathons or do Crossfit, but I often trod 15,000 steps a day according to the hand-me-down pedometer Suze had given me. I'd just hurried, for Lynn's sake. "Can I see her?"

"Absolutely not."

"What harm can she do?" A gruff voice sounded behind me.

"I know she looks small, Sir. But she can do more harm than you can possibly imagine."

Ignoring Cesar, I turned and found a middle-aged bald man. A bristly salt-and-pepper mustache bisected his wide face. His name tag read *Capt. Robert Tang.*

"You're the priest from St. Giles?" He looked me up and down, which never takes long when you're five feet on a good day.

"Alma Lee." I extended my hand. "How certain are you that she did it?"

"Rob Tang." He shook my hand, then glanced at Cesar, whose face went artfully neutral. "We are investigating all possibilities."

Not sure of a damn thing, then. Which meant there was a possibility that Lynn had not murdered her wife. Thank God.

"The suspect is very distraught. Maybe you can calm her down enough that she'll be able to tell us what happened? Acting as a sort of ad hoc police chaplain."

"I'd be delighted to try." In fact, hadn't I used that very phrase with Jenny just the other day? Still, it seemed odd Tang was so willing to let me meddle.

Cesar glowered and pointed at the purple stole draped over my arm. "What's that for?"

"Confession. Well, technically we call it the Rite of Reconciliation, but it's the same—"

"Oh, no. Oh, hell no. If she told you anything it would be—"

"Yep. Between her, me, and God."

"I forbid you from hearing that woman's confession."

"First off, as if you can forbid me anything. Second, your captain asked me to help." I flapped the stole.

"Come on, Garza," Tang said. "You're a good Catholic boy. You know if the suspect gets right with God, she'll feel compelled to tell the truth. Let's give Reverend Lee here a chance." Captain Tang gallantly took my hand and winked at Cesar. Did he know we'd been an item?

My boots clapped against the square terra cotta tiles. Pairs of gray desks faced each other, some messy, some tidy, some so bare as to indicate a vacancy in the department. A glass-walled room in the corner housed a rolling white board, busy with a collage of images, Cesar's scrawled script, and arrows connecting things.

It had to be the murder room, the evidence gathered in Cindy's case all on display. Could I slip in there and snap a photo of what they'd discovered with my phone?

"Don't even think about it," a low voice rumbled in my ears.

"Think about what? I was just admiring the walls. This shade of beige paint really dresses up the cinderblocks. And the maroon trim. Very homicidal. I mean, suitable for the homicide squad."

At my side, Captain Tang chuckled. "Is she always like this?"

"An exhausting twenty-four seven, Sir."

Well, if Tang hadn't known before, Cesar had revealed we used to be together around the clock. If memory served, it was not my meddling that had kept us both awake.

Suddenly, I realized how close he was, and my back tingled from my scalp to my Achilles heels. Oh, God, please give Naomi a nudge my way so I could stop thinking about this man.

Captain Tang opened a door, leading into a small dark room. On the wall, a one-way mirror revealed Lynn hunched over a table, her hair a scraggly curtain covering her face. Through that veil, I saw her lips moving like someone reciting fervent prayers.

"What's she saying?"

"She's talking to Cindy." Cesar pressed his back to the wall and crossed his arms. "Apparently, you said in your sermon yesterday you talk to her, too."

Ah. It suddenly made sense why Tang had agreed to let me in. He believed I'd contributed to her troubled state of mind.

"Is she having a psychotic break?"

Cesar frowned. "The social worker doesn't think so. She's lucid, but she won't respond to our questions."

"Lawyer?"

Captain Tang reached for the doorknob. "She doesn't want a lawyer. Cesar called a public defender, and she told the poor woman to get out. Questioning her when she's like this won't hold up in court. So right now, I count you as our best option.

"Okay. I'll try." I stepped into the hallway. Cesar followed, then let me into Lynn's room. The door clicked shut behind me. I faced the one-way mirror, knowing they observed from the other side.

When I turned to Lynn, I found her watching me through her hair, smiling eerily. "Hey, look who's here, Cindy. It's Alma."

She tilted her head expectantly.

"Hi, Lynn."

"Ssh. Cindy's talking to you."

Um. Right. And the social worker had deemed this a normal psychological state? Dear God, compared to what?

"What's she saying, Lynn?"

"She's saying I didn't kill her."

"Oh. Can she tell us who did?" I had to ask, on the off-chance Lynn was conducting a legit séance in the interview room.

Lynn shook her head, a quick burst of small movements that would surely rattle her brain. "No. No. That's not important right now."

Cesar might beg to differ, but he stood on the other side of that one-way mirror so his opinion didn't count.

"Okay. What is important?"

"Cindy wants to tell you what she did." Lynn tipped her head to the left as if pointing to the invisible ghost of her wife.

Should I pretend I saw her? I tried looking at the spot and giggled.

Lynn kicked me under the table. "This is no time for laughing."

"Ow." I rubbed my shin. "That hurt."

She crossed her arms.

Fair point—I hadn't been murdered or held under suspicion of committing murder. My shin stopped smarting. Maybe if I'd brought her some chocolate, she'd have been nicer to me.

"What does Cindy want to tell me, Lynn?"

"She wants you to know what she did to make me so mad."

I couldn't help it. I glanced over my shoulder at the one-way mirror. "Lynn, do you want me to put on my stole and make this a formal confession? Then whatever you say is only between you, me, and God."

She waved her arm, dismissing my caution. "She wants to tell you she took all our savings and dumped the money I'd saved for fertility treatment into that bottomless shit hole of a bar."

My stomach sank. I'd wondered how Cindy was still buying liquor, paying her staff and utilities. Whenever I'd asked, she'd vaguely replied, "loans."

"How much money?"

"All together, one hundred sixty thousand dollars. My entire savings plus my inheritance from my grandmother. All gone." Lynn's words came out sharper and more clearly. Her crazy act seemed to recede.

I restrained myself from whistling at the hefty sum. "What did you do when you found out?"

"What any sane person would do. I kicked her out and called a lawyer."

Damn. Cindy hadn't told me any of this.

"But she wasn't on my couch for most of the last two weeks. You let her come back?"

Lynn nodded. "We tried to talk it out, but once I'd learned about the money, I couldn't stuff a single grievance back down. Every hurt I'd tried to forgive and forget suddenly had its own memorial marble statue in my brain."

I barked out a hoarse laugh. Lynn sounded far more like herself.

"That night, she invited me to the closing party, but I didn't want to step into that place. It was a black hole that had swallowed up my savings and my marriage." Her voice cracked on the last word. "And I was right. It even took her in the end."

"But you left work early, drove across the bridge. Did you go looking for her at the bar?"

Lynn sniffed. Her angry expression cracked, revealing the grief in her sunken eyes. "We'd fought that afternoon. She wasn't answering my calls or texts, and I was getting frantic—you know the feeling?—mad and scared shitless at the same time."

"Yep." When Cesar had graduated from the academy and worked patrol, I had felt it every time he was a little late and didn't text.

"I drove by the bar, but it was dark. I figured she'd gone to your place or out to an all-night club. And I was spitting mad at her for not even telling me which one." She dropped her forehead to the table, hard. "She was probably already dead on the steps of St. Giles', and I drove right by, madder than hell and thinking the worst of her."

Cindy had stolen Lynn's savings, her hopes and dreams. She was entitled to think the worst.

Lynn raised her head and sucked in a gasping breath. "I asked Cesar how she got from the bar to the steps of St. Giles'."

"What did he say?"

"She crawled. There was gravel in her palms, but somehow she made it that far with a fatal head wound." Lynn's voice trembled.

Had she been trying to reach me for help? The friend who'd abandoned her, just across the street, but too far to save her. A surge of yesterday's nausea rose up in me. I inhaled through my nose and refocused on Lynn.

"Did anyone see you?"

"I went to Happy Donuts on Church at 1 a.m. We ate there on our second date. And I paid for my éclair with a credit card."

"Did you try calling her?"

"Like a million times and left that many voicemails, too."

Those probably proved nothing, but it made me more inclined to believe her. Had the police accessed Cindy's phone records and listened to the messages?

"I'm so glad you came," she said. "After your sermon, I knew you would understand this guilt I feel. The last things we said to each other were so awful…"

"And yet, she's here now to hear you, right?"

"Well… She is, but only in my imagination."

Tension melted from my shoulders. "I'm of the opinion that all human contact with the dead is in our imagination, but that doesn't mean it's not real. That's just how we access God and her dimensions." I reached across the table for her hands and she clasped mine, hot and firm. "Tell Cindy you're sorry, and if you're ready, you can say you forgive her, too."

She nodded her head vigorously. "I am."

I led her in a prayer—not a confessional one, but one for peace and reconciliation. She stumbled on the words, "I forgive you," but she repeated them firmly a second time. After our amen, she sat, eyes closed and taking long, steady breaths. I watched the peace settle over her, like something sprinkled from above, changing her very composition.

"Now, I want you to call a lawyer."

The door burst open. "No need for a lawyer. You're free to go."

"What?" Lynn blinked, voicing my question. Nothing she said proved her innocence. Unless…

"You have another suspect?" One with more than circumstantial proof.

"Just don't leave town, Lynn."

She pulled back to stand up, but I kept hold of her hands. "When you're feeling a little better, let's talk about your mom project. It doesn't have to cost a hundred thousand dollars."

I didn't possess even a minuscule DNA sequence of maternal instinct, but the Bible had taught me having that particular longing denied could slowly crush a woman. If motherhood called to Lynn, I would help her find a way.

She squeezed her eyes closed and nodded. At the door to the interview room, she hugged me. "Thank you. And thanks for keeping an eye on Cesar. With you on the case, I'm sure justice will be served."

Apparently Lynn also read too many of those detective-priest whodunits. I was proving no help at all. Still, I returned her embrace. "Is your sister still at your place?"

"Yeah. I can call her to come—"

"Let's not put her out. I'll have someone drive you home." Captain Tang offered Lynn his arm. He led her to that pert blonde who'd been with Mario the night of the party. She smiled at Lynn, her eyes holding just the right amount of sympathy. If she wasn't careful to hide that skill, she'd always get slapped with death-notice duty.

"Well." I sidestepped around Cesar, "Happy to be of assistance."

"Not so fast." Despite being twice as big as me, the man was fast. He blocked my escape and herded me into the interview room.

Chapter Thirteen

My collar felt too tight, and sweat prickled in my armpits. I've never owned a car, but I'd slapped many *Question Authority* bumper stickers onto the outside of BART trains in my rambunctious youth.

What's that—I still seem rambunctious to you? Why, thank you. Am I blushing?

In a split second, with the door slamming closed on the interview room, Cesar ceased to be my oldest friend and ex-lover. He represented Authority with a capital A, and I grew spines.

Then he propped one hip on the table and opened a folder. He didn't ask me to sit.

My spines retracted. Perhaps porcupine-mode had been a bit of an overreaction.

"That was Naomi Cohen coming to meet you for breakfast, wasn't it?"

Okay—best not to lower *all* my defenses. I may still need the sharp tips of my bristles out.

"Yes."

"How did you meet her?"

"She's a rabbi." Not a lie, just an evasion. "We're colleagues."

"She's very beautiful." His coffee-brown eyes cut into me.

I could say I hadn't noticed, but demurring probably wouldn't soften the tension in the cell-sized room.

"Yes, she is."

"Are you seeing her?"

"Is that a personal or professional question?"

"Her brother is our number-one suspect. The evidence against

Lynn is circumstantial, but we've got material stuff on Cohen. I think you should stay away from her until the case is closed."

"Why?"

"Does she know that you know me?"

I shrugged. "So."

"Did it occur to you she might be using you to help her brother?"

In fact, that had been her goal. But I hadn't seen it as using, so much as asking, as forming a friendship, one that might develop into something more with the first person I'd wanted since the man not quite interrogating me.

I glanced at the mirror. Was the captain watching me through the glass? I reached around to the back of my neck and sprung my clerical collar free. Cesar and I exhaled at the same time. He'd never gotten used to the thing. I set it on the table.

By opening his folder, he'd exposed a photo. In the sepia tones cast by the yellow street lamps at the 16th St. BART Plaza, a camera had captured David Cohen mid-step. He wore a puffy jacket, his long curls blowing high. At the bottom of the print, a time signature in vintage digital-alarm-clock font read *TH JUN 1 12:43 AM*.

"Shit." I picked it up and examined his shoes—were they the missing pair? The print revealed no details other than the color black. But perhaps the digital version would be in higher resolution.

"Things aren't looking good for the rabbi's brother."

"He loves kittens."

Cesar crossed his arms and tilted his head. "She told you that?"

My failure to reply was its own answer.

"Shit, is right, Alls. Her brother's in deep. Wait until the case is closed, and see if she still wants to have breakfast with you, okay?"

Genuine concern rumbled in his voice, but it didn't temper my anger at him. "No, it's not okay. How about, instead, you mind your own business?"

"This happens all the time." His voice remained calm, not even a click louder. "Ask anybody out there." He flung his arm toward the desks down the hall. "Girls meet a cop at the bar, screw them like crazy, and in the morning ask to get a few parking tickets taken care of."

"She's not some femme fatale, you dummy. She's new in town,

and she needs a friend. We have a lot in common."

"Uh huh."

"Not everybody's a user, Cesar."

"Nope. Not everybody. Some people have savior complexes instead."

"Riiiight. But help me out. I'm a little confused whether those wannabe saviors become cops or priests."

"Touché." Cesar chuckled.

Making him laugh still warmed me from the inside, apparently. It definitely diffused my anger.

"So, Alma, what did Naomi tell you about her brother?"

"Oh. Not much. I'm sure it's nothing a master detective like you hasn't already figured out."

"Try me."

"Well, how about you tell me what you've learned, and I'll add anything else she's shared?"

"How about you stop screwing around, Alls? If you withhold evidence, it will be out of my hands. Tang will throw the book at you."

Another day, I'd have teased him for using such a cop-show cliché. On this occasion, I had to keep him from noticing how sweaty my palms had gotten. I crammed them into the back pockets of my jeans.

"She told me his marriage is in trouble and that he's probably having an affair with a younger woman."

"Yeah. Got that already. What else?"

"He put all his money into getting the bar started. He stood to lose a lot if Cindy refused to vacate."

"Yeah, yeah. What else?"

"Nothing."

"What about that night? Did she really not hear anything?

"That's what she told me."

"Is she a light sleeper?" he asked.

"I wouldn't know."

"Come on, Alma. We're talking about a woman's life. If he gets away with murder, he'll do it again."

This was it. The moment I could tell the truth about the missing shoes, or I could try to buy Naomi and David more time. But for what? To exonerate him, or so he could disappear to South America forever?

"What's your evidence against Cohen?"

Cesar inflated his cheeks and blew out the breath slowly, glaring at me with narrowed eyes. "Footprint at the scene in his shoe size. In Cindy's blood."

I cringed, even though I already knew. Cesar reached for my shoulder.

I retreated before he made contact. "And did you find the bloody shoe?"

Jaw clenched, he jerked his head to the right. "No."

"Well, if he's your man, I guess you better ask yourself where those shoes could be, between the plaza," I pointed at the photo, "and his flat."

"What are you saying?"

"I'm saying your uniforms need to search the neighborhood. Unless there's a camera on every block?" I raised my brows, already knowing the answer.

In spite of what happened to Yeye, my parents are privacy nuts. They hate surveillance cameras in public. Whenever we walk by the BART Plaza, my mother whispers vehemently, *El Hermano Mayor está mirando.* And she avoids public transportation because of the closed- circuit cameras on municipal busses and trains. No Uber either—then the cell phones and satellites track where you are.

What my mother thinks Big Brother will catch her doing, I can't even imagine. Buying contraband raw milk for the grocery store? She's hardly organizing a revolution—she leaves that to me.

"There are no city cameras on the streets around his flat." Cesar's eyes didn't relax into their natural, almond shape, and he pursed his lips.

I clapped my hands together. "Then it sounds like it's time for some old-fashioned police work." I put my hand on the doorknob. He didn't stop me. I turned and, all casual like, posed a question. "Would you mind telling me what the murderer hit Cindy with?"

"Why?"

"Oh, you know, so I can keep my eyes peeled. Was it the candlestick, the rope, the lead pipe?" I wracked my brain trying to think of the other weapons in the board game Clue that could be used to bludgeon. "Crystal decanter?" No, that wasn't one.

Still, his eyes widened, just a millimeter. I'd suck at interrogating anybody but him.

"Or was it a liquor bottle off the bar shelf?"

"Goddammit, Alma."

I winced. It's hard to offend me, but that swear word does—it's so careless and unnecessary. Isn't it enough to damn something yourself, without asking the creator of everything to reject some part of her creation? And Cesar knew how I felt, but this time he didn't smooth away his offense with an apology.

I twisted the knob.

"Wait."

I let it spring back into place and turned. His remorse was written in the angle of his brows.

"I just hate it when you... "A frustrated sound came from the back of his throat.

I laughed. "Yeah. I hate it when you—" I mimicked the sound, "me too."

The one-upping, the unwelcome mind-reading—the cost of knowing each other too well, or maybe the cost of failing to compromise and make room for the one you loved most. It didn't hurt as much as it grated against me, like he was covered in coarse sand.

He stepped closer. "Seriously, Alls. You cannot tell anyone that detail. If it gets out, it could blow the investigation. For Cindy's sake, do not blab that over pillow talk with Naomi."

"Roger, Detective Garza."

I dashed out, heading straight for David Cohen's place.

Chapter Fourteen

Halfway to the apartment Naomi shared with her brother, I realized my mistake. What could I say? Your brother did it, and the cops know. That would not go well. Better to wait it out, let her come to me for comfort instead. I headed to my office to do the work that paid my bills.

Five days after the murder, every time I approached the church behind which I lived, I still had to avert my gaze from the stoop where I'd found Cindy. Hopefully, when the case was solved, I'd be able to make eye contact with the doorway again.

Kayla hopped up and waved a pile of yellow message slips at me. She was twenty-two and more tech savvy than half of Google's employees, but she preferred to use the carbon copy forms, torn out of a spiral notebook. I think she believed the stacks would convince me to spend more time at my desk, or somehow propel me toward a come-to-Jesus moment about my lack of organization.

She refused to understand my preference for disorder was a spiritual choice. It left me open to hear God's call out of the chaos.

"Al has been trying to reach you all day. He says it's urgent."

Maybe he'd taken Jenny Wong's advice and decided it couldn't wait until lunch on Thursday. Was today the day to read aloud his litany of complaints against me? I did not feel the Holy Spirit tugging me to respond, so I put his message on the bottom of the pile.

"And someone called from Good Sam. Your healthcare for the homeless task force met this morning and you no-showed without telling anyone."

Crap. I scrolled through the notifications on my phone. There it was—a reminder that I must have completely ignored while I was in the police station. I'd need to write some groveling emails to apologize for my truancy on a committee I'd urged the hospital to form.

I flipped through the stack of messages as I walked toward my office. Three down, Kayla had written-screamed, *BISHOP'S OFFICE. PHONE IMMEDIATELY.*

Why were they calling? Was this about my continuing education form? I'd filled it out, but had I sent it?

I glanced at my desk. Oh, hell...

Kayla had organized my scribbled notes, the articles I'd printed out, my church leadership books open face down on the desk. In neat piles, the whole seemed far less than the sum of its parts. I eyed the recycle bin. Had Kayla deemed some of my papers disposable?

If so, she'd been sneaky. The bin was empty.

I clenched my teeth and mentally chanted a mantra. *Thou shalt not murder. Thou shalt not murder.* Then I remembered her holding my hair back while I vomited, calling my mom and Cesar out of concern for me. My ballistic rage subsided, giving way to domestic-grade irritation.

Stacked up together, the pile of yellow message slips teetered precariously. Gently, I laid the new messages atop and picked up the phone to call the bishop.

"Jenny just emailed to say the newsletter copy is due in an hour," Kayla shouted from her desk.

I bit my tongue instead of biting her head off about messing with my desk.

I dashed off an article describing our upcoming volunteer day at the food bank. Since I had the church calendar open, I wrote blurbs about our twenty-somethings social on Saturday, the mobile homeless shelter that would rotate through our parish hall next week, and a request for more volunteers to visit the housebound in our neighborhood. Then I picked up my phone—wait, who had I been about to call?

I glanced at the message pile. Kayla had scrawled Al's name on the top slip. Okay, perhaps the Holy Spirit *was* nudging me to call him. I dialed his number. The line went to voicemail, so I left him a message.

"Your one o'clock is here," Kayla called.

I had a one o'clock? Crap. I checked my calendar on my computer. No appointment filled that slot. The tower of messages tottered, reminding me of a famous Biblical tower—Babel—which symbolized human vanity and ambition. Perhaps Kayla had a point.

I popped up from my desk. In the front office stood the adorable boys who ran the vegan restaurant/laundromat down the street. The last time I'd dropped in for bean and cashew-cheese enchiladas and to wash my clerical shirts, they'd announced their engagement and asked if I'd do their wedding. Apparently I'd been enjoying my margarita too much to bother recording our first premarital counseling appointment.

Perfect. I smeared a smile on my face and stuck my head out the door.

"Alma, look at you!" Rick pinched my waist. "You haven't been eating enough." Bald and bearded, he'd developed a belly as the chef-half of their endeavor.

The trim, fashionable Martín swatted Rick's hand. "Leave her alone. Just because you're gay doesn't mean you get to grope." He turned to me and rolled his eyes. "I swear, he's so handsy with women." Leaning in to kiss my cheek he said, "Those lace-ups are to die for."

We both looked at my burgundy military-style ankle boots. Feminine, but with a tough edge, the way I liked to think of myself. For some reason, the thought called to mind Cesar punching me. *Alma Lee does not get hysterical.*

My throat tightened, and the silence stretched out into an awkward pause. What had he said? Oh, yes, my boots. "Thanks. Come on in."

Kayla had attacked the surface of my desk, but she hadn't gotten to all the objects I'd stacked in the two chairs facing it. Quickly I moved my communion visiting kit and the stole I'd taken to the police station from one, the facedown Biblical commentary open to Sunday's lessons from the other.

"Here. Have a seat."

The boys had already booked a wedding date with Kayla. We discussed the plan for premarital counseling. Back in seminary, I scoffed at using an online inventory to guide premarital counseling. I'd become a believer when one had accurately predicted my friend Jordan was a perfect match for our ethics prof, now her husband, Dominic Lawrence, in nearly every way. With my help, they'd remedied their area of incompatibility and made me godmother to their daughter in thanks.

Rick, Martín, and I discussed the process, got them set up to take the online inventories, and booked another date to meet in two weeks. This one I remembered to record in my calendar. After they left, I'd be sure to have Kayla pat me on the back.

Martín stood and closed his jacket at the second button down. "Could we pop into the church? My mom is sending me magazine clippings of flower arrangements. I'd like to snap photos of the space, to get her off my back."

"Sure." This time I remembered to check my watch. I needed to be at Lois's apartment in fifteen minutes, but it was just around the corner. I could let them into the sanctuary, then be on my way.

We rounded the building, and I glanced up the stairs. A long lump under blankets lay at the top. My heart raced. I grabbed Rick's elbow for support.

Oh, sweet baby Jesus, no. I could not handle another corpse on the church steps.

The lump emitted a snuffling sound, followed by a single loud snore. I released Rick's arm and straightened my spine, casting a quick glance over my shoulder to make sure no one had seen me freaking out, especially not Cesar.

"Just give me a second. It's probably Phil. He's our regular afternoon napper. Harmless, but he doesn't like being woken up." I even recognized his gray woolen blanket, standard issue of the San Francisco Night Ministry. But those shoes sticking out from under the charcoal fabric were new.

They read *SCAMPER* in red across the center of the sole. Where would Phil get a pair of two hundred-dollar shoes? The back of my neck tingled. I ascended the stairs and bent for a closer look. Sporty black wingtips with horizontal lines for tread, barely worn. Some dark substance had seeped between the still-new rubber lines on the toe-end of the right shoe. Sleeping rough in the Mission, the mystery substance could be anything. Ketchup smeared on the sidewalk next to a hotdog vendor. Dirty motor oil pooled in a crosswalk.

Or, it could be Cindy's blood on David's shoe.

I called Cesar.

"What now?" he growled in greeting.

"Come to St. Giles'. Bring an evidence bag, and a spare pair of men's shoes."

"Damn. On my way."

I had to hand it to him—when it mattered, he trusted me without question.

At the bottom of the stairs, Rick frowned up at me. Martín twisted his watch on his wrist.

"Hey guys, this may take a while. Can I show you the church next time?"

Rick eyed Phil and nodded vigorously. Martín's mouth was a thin line.

"Send your mom the link to our website. The photos of the interior will put her at ease."

His shoulders fell, and he exhaled. "Sounds good. See you in a couple weeks."

"Have fun doing your relationship inventories." I tried for a light tone.

They both waggled their fingers at me, then headed south toward their laundro-restaurant.

I sat on the bottom step. Moments later, Cesar pulled up in his SUV, a patrol car right behind him.

I pointed at Phil. "I think those might be the shoes you're looking for."

He tilted his head. "Damn."

The patrol officers came to Cesar's side.

He pointed toward Phil. "We need those shoes. They're possibly evidence in a homicide. And we need to question this guy—"

"Phil. His name is Phil. He likes it if you sing 'Rise and Shine' when you wake him up."

"You heard the lady." Cesar shrugged.

He turned back to me with brown eyes blazing. "What, exactly, did Naomi tell you?"

At the top of the stairs, a female officer roused Phil gently, using his name. He handled it better than on some days—only swatting and cursing, no shouting or kicking. As I'd suggested, the older policeman began to sing, and the transient man calmed right down.

I blew out a breath. "She told me you'd examined David's shoes."

Cesar nodded slowly, patiently. I sensed the caged fury beneath the gesture. "If that were all she'd said, you'd never know that the shoes we wanted had horizontal-lined tread. What else did she tell you, Alma?" On the question, his upbeat tone turned shrill.

Muscles tightened all the way down my spine. I'd really pissed him off.

"That a pair of his shoes was missing. Scampers."

"But you didn't see fit to tell me that, while they both acted as if all his shoes were right there, failing my luminal test?"

"She thinks he's innocent."

"I don't." He sharpened his already razor-edged gaze on me.

"Look, I don't know. I see your side on this. He looks guilty as hell. But she knows him… "

"Nobody's sister thinks they're cold blooded until they find out the—"

"Boss?" An officer approached gingerly, like even a firm footfall might trigger Cesar's rage.

"What?" he barked.

"Phil has seven-hundred dollars cash in his coat pocket."

Cesar whistled. "Denomination?"

"Ones, fives, tens and twenties. Nothing higher."

"What does that mean?" I asked.

"Contents of a cash register," replied the officer. "Very likely The Carlos Club's."

Cesar had turned his back on me. I elbowed my way into the conversation. "I thought it wasn't a robbery."

Cesar glared at the officer, who blushed. "Sorry."

This changed everything! David had no motive to steal a handful of petty cash.

"Why didn't you tell me?" I blurted.

Cesar jerked his head, dismissing the officer, and shot me an impatient glare. "Because well-meaning meddlers can mess up murder investigations."

"Yeah. I bet it's annoying when they find the evidence you've been seeking for days."

"Lucky coincidence."

He was likely right, but I couldn't let him win the argument.

"What's lucky is that I know everybody and see everything that happens in this neighborhood. You should consult with me all the time, like Scotland Yard and Sherlock Holmes."

"Lord, help me." Cesar looked up to heaven.

Uh oh. I'd pushed him pretty far, if he was petitioning the God he didn't believe in for help.

"What about the tea? Did the lab send you results?"

He grabbed a fistful of his hair, his shoulders lifting halfway to his ears, and spoke through clenched teeth. "Yes."

"It's a traditional blend, like you said—"

"Told you—"

"But someone packed it with a second traditional blend called *gua di san*." He labored carefully over the unfamiliar syllables. "It's an emetic, meant to purge you of toxins."

I felt my brows furrow. "Someone wanted to make me sick?"

"So it seems. Or it was a very clumsy poisoning attempt."

I crossed my arms. "If someone was trying to scare me off, they don't know me very well." And they'd labeled the tea tin for *Mother Alma*, a form of address my acquaintances knew I despised. Could that have been David's doing? Did he know about *gua di san* or only about mixing cocktails? And if I asked Naomi, would she tell me the truth, or omit it the way she'd neglected to tell Cesar about her brother's missing shoes?

"Detective?" An officer called to Cesar from where he stood next to Phil, who sat on the ground near the patrol car.

The transient's filthy bare feet jutted out, and he rested his forehead on his raised knees. I followed Cesar over, ignoring the surly set of his jaw. If he really wanted me to leave, he would have insisted. Maybe he saw the merits of my consulting-detective argument. And that vomit-inducing tea made the case even more personal.

"No, man, I didn't go nowhere near The Carlos Club. Guys aren't welcome there, you know what I mean?"

"Then where did your pocket full of cash come from?"

"That's my business, man."

"And where did you get those sweet kicks, Phil?" Cesar asked.

"Found 'em."

"Where?"

Phil frowned and scratched his head through hair as thick and black as Cesar's, but dull with dirt. "Can't remember."

"If they turn out to have a murder victim's blood on them, you best remember quickly."

"Blood?" Phil's Adam's apple bobbed. "Naw man. I didn't see

any blood. Alma, tell them. I'm not like that. I don't hurt nobody."

Cesar looked at me. "How well do you know Phil, here?"

I shrugged. Not enough to be a character reference. And he did get belligerent about being woken up, but I'd never known him to be truly violent. It came down to how desperate a person was for cash, which depended on what they planned to buy with said cash.

I'd always assumed Phil was a drinker. I looked him over—no track marks, no scabs on his face, and for a guy living on the street, his pearly whites looked pretty darn good. To erase all doubt, he burped a cloud of gas that smelled like the storage room of The Carlos Club—stale beer.

All of us retreated a step. Phil winced, apologetic that he'd offended our noses. He had such soulful eyes, like he'd seen worlds of pain I couldn't even imagine. And I have a very vivid imagination.

My belly tingled with certainty. No way could he have bludgeoned Cindy for the contents of a cash register. Was this that cop's intuition thing? Or the same conviction that Naomi felt about David?

But she couldn't see the facts clearly. She could only see her kitten-loving baby brother.

Cesar extended a hand to help Phil stand. "Come on. We're gonna take you over to the station, see if we can help you remember where you got those shoes and that wad of cash." His steady, polite tone put me at ease, in spite of my general distrust of authority. Cesar was honorable. No one would hurt Phil to get answers, and the evidence would likely lead them all right back to David Cohen.

I would wait and hope Naomi would count me as a friend, or more, once the truth was out.

Chapter Fifteen

My phone rang. The screen read Jenny Wong.

"This is Alma."

"Where are you?" she whispered.

"Uh. At church?" The police were helping Phil into the back seat of the patrol car.

From behind his steering wheel, Cesar raised his hand in farewell, then peeled out.

"I'm at Lois's apartment. Why aren't you?"

Crap. Was it two o'clock already?

"She called me in a panic when you hadn't arrived, and Kayla said you vanished from the office half an hour ago. I canceled a meeting with my campaign manager to run over here."

Thank God somebody had her back, since Kayla clearly didn't. "Okay. I'm on my way right now. Thanks for the call."

I popped in to tell Kayla where I was going. "And next time when someone calls and you don't know where I am, say 'she had to step out.' Not 'I have no idea where she's gone now.' Then call my cell."

Her jaw set.

I held my arms loose at my sides so I didn't cross them. "Kayla, you cannot passive-aggressive me into obeying your organizational system. It pains me to say this because you are an excellent parish administrator, and you were very kind when I was sick. But if you hate working for me, it's time to find another job. Otherwise, I need you to accept that a level of chaos is my style. It's what makes me effective."

With her teeth clenched so tightly, she apparently couldn't

speak, she nodded.

Ten minutes later, I reached Lois's building on Twenty-Second and Dolores. I rang the bell and someone buzzed me in.

Lois opened the door to her flat and hugged me. "Oh, Alma, thank goodness. When Kayla said you'd vanished, I feared the Fourteenth Street Killer had struck again, so I called Jenny to see if she knew where you were."

"The Fourteenth Street Killer?" I hadn't heard that one yet.

"That's what they're calling him on the neighborhood message boards."

Good news. After the onion flavored communion bread incident, I hadn't expected Lois could read well enough to keep on top of the neighborhood message boards.

"Come in, come in. Jenny's just made tea."

I followed Lois into her kitchen, where Jenny was setting down a tray of meringues, which were obviously not vegan. If restaurateurs like Rick made it easy to be vegan, rejecting the hospitality of sweet old ladies was definitely the hardest part.

"Thanks for calling, Jenny."

She looked at me but didn't smile, her jaw set much like Kayla's had been just minutes ago.

I needed to offer an explanation. "Something came up with the investigation, and I was helping the police."

"No problem, dear. You just sit right here." Lois pulled a chair out for me. "I know how busy you are."

We sat together at the table and I gently prodded Lois for information about her eyesight. Had she seen the ophthalmologist lately? Did she feel safe on the stairs or out and about in the neighborhood?

From what I observed and how she described her routines, the onion bread incident had probably been a one-off, not a sign of major decline. She seemed comfortably independent.

She vanished into her bedroom to search for a photo she wanted to show us, leaving Jenny and me alone.

"Alma, this has to stop," my junior warden whispered. "I can't keep covering for you when you miss meetings because you're off doing God knows what."

God did know and, as far as I could tell, had a gentle hand in guiding my activities. "I was helping the police."

"Right. They always appreciate nosy citizens assisting with their murder investigations."

Ouch. When Cesar said it, I didn't mind so much. Ribbing each other was our Olympic sport. I opened my mouth to tell her about the shoes and cash on Phil as a defense for my involvement. But that would thoroughly piss off Cesar. What if she mentioned those details to someone at City Hall or to a concerned constituent?

So I took another tack. "Cindy was a close friend, and she died on the steps of our church. There have been several matters the police needed my help with."

"And meanwhile, you can't be bothered to call Al back."

"I did—"

"I warned you he thinks you're a scatterbrain, Alma, that you don't focus enough on your job and your parishioners. And you keep proving him right."

"That's not true." In fact, I'd gotten lots of work done in the hour I'd sat at my desk this morning. And I didn't agree in the slightest with Al's definition of the boundaries of my job. St. Giles' was vibrant because it opened its doors to the neighborhood. We couldn't slam them shut when something tragic and violent happened right outside.

Lois reappeared. "It took me a while to find it." She laid a newspaper clipping on the table. "Here's my Benjamin receiving the Friends of Families award twenty years ago." It was the same award Jenny had received Wednesday night.

My warden gazed at the photo, her stern expression softening into a smile. "How wonderful, Lois. It was quite an honor."

"And did you enjoy the party?" Lois poured us more tea—black instead of my preferred green, but the caffeine was welcome. "Benjamin never liked those galas, but I loved getting dressed up."

Jenny chuckled. "I have to say, I'm with Benjamin. My feet hurt terribly after a night in high heels. But the events increase awareness of issues like homeless families, so it's worth it."

She went on to talk about the work Friends of Families was doing with so much passion that my defensiveness melted away. Jenny improved the lives of the city's disadvantaged residents every day, and she was only trying to help me succeed at St. Giles.

Her frustration that she kept getting called when I missed an appointment was warranted. For that matter, so was Kayla's. My parish administrator and I needed to find some kind of organizational compromise so she wasn't perpetually frustrated by my unexplained comings and goings.

Before I left, I grabbed another moment alone with Jenny. "I hear your concerns, and I will connect with Al right away."

"Good." She patted my shoulder. "I'm sure we can work all this out."

I hoofed it back to the office to make peace with Kayla. Perhaps it was time to relent to her request I use clearly labeled trays to sort my papers. Last time she'd raised the issue, I'd said, "I find your systems of categorization arbitrary."

Kayla had stomped back to her desk and shouted. "Just because you like to defy categorization doesn't mean it's useless to sort out things you want to read from things you have to do."

At the time, I'd remained stuck on the ideological issue. People are people, papers are papers; there's no need to label. Now, I saw the flaw in that logic. Papers aren't people. Perhaps it would work better to impose organization on them.

Contrite, I slipped through the front door of St. Giles' and offered up my office as a sacrifice to Kayla. She drew out the paper trays she'd stashed under her desk in hopes this day would come. We set to work, chatting about how we might better manage my calendar together. Going forward, I promised to tell her where I was when the Holy Spirit decided to blow me where she would, and I chose to follow.

The organizational project distracted me from thoughts of Phil, David Cohen, and Naomi wracked with fear for her brother.

When they intruded, I shoved them from my mind. The people of St. Giles' needed me to be their priest, not off pretending I was Miss Marple.

I called Al again. He didn't answer.

When Kayla left at five, I clocked out, too, ready for a night in and a little TV binging self-care. I changed into PJs, popped popcorn for dinner, and crawled under a mohair throw Hazel had knitted me. Cueing up *Will & Grace* reminded me of Lynn, and I dialed her number.

Her sister answered. "Yeah, she's right here. Let me get her for you."

The phone made swishing sounds as it changed hands. "Hey, Alma."

"Hey, there. How are you?"

"Better. Better. Thanks for calling. Any news on the case?"

I opened my mouth, then remembered I shouldn't reveal anything. "Cesar's working hard. He's bound to wrap it up soon."

"Yeah. He's not so bad, huh?"

"He's all right."

"Actually, he was good. Really kind."

That was Cesar, but I couldn't let him ruin his own reputation. "Don't let that fool you. He was just playing good cop."

"Yeah." Lynn chuckled. "Probably."

"Hey, I was serious about your mom project. When you're ready, I'm here to help."

"Thanks. And I've been thinking about the funeral and what Cindy would want. She wasn't that religious, but I've been asking her, the way you suggested, and we have some ideas."

"Great."

"So, once the case is closed and they give her back…" Lynn choked on her words.

I hadn't realized the medical examiner still had her body. "We'll do it when you're ready. When it's time. There's no hurry."

"Okay." She sniffed loudly.

"Listen, I don't know about you, but I'm in serious need of a TV marathon. Call me if you need me."

"I don't know how to thank you for coming to the station today. I feel… more at peace."

See, that's what comes of letting the Holy Spirit guide you?

"Good. Sleep well." I ended the call, pulled my blanket up to under my chin, and pressed play.

Chapter Sixteen

After Morning Prayer the next day, I sat at my frighteningly clean desk and tried not to hyperventilate. Where did I start? It was so much easier to tackle the item on the top of the pile, put out the most urgent fire.

A clean desk required... strategy, prioritization. How did one decide between so many urgent tasks and important issues?

Perhaps giving in to Kayla had been a mistake. I preferred the I-smell-smoke method of discernment.

Also, I wanted to call Naomi like I craved my first cup of green tea in the morning. But I'd told Cesar about David's shoes. Would she forgive me for revealing her secret and finding the crucial evidence against her brother?

The top message on my neatly paper-weighted pile of yellow slips was the one from Al, which I'd already tried to return. I called him again.

"Hello?" A woman's voice answered, and she sounded too young to be his wife.

"Hi, this is Alma Lee. I'm Al's priest from St. Giles'. Is he there?"

"Oh, hi. I'm Sydney, his daughter. You must have heard the news."

The ever-present lump in my throat swelled. Twice people had said this to me about their recently deceased loved ones as if God sent carrier pigeons from heaven directly to the priest when someone in the congregation died. Or maybe they thought we received the message psychically. Needless to say, ESP is not one of my spiritual gifts.

Also, I did not want Al, the note-taking-curmudgeon, to be dead. He was a well-meaning thorn in my side. I glanced up at the white ceiling. *Hey, Holy Trinity, can St. Giles' get a grace period down here? I need at least three months after Cindy before I can handle another death.*

"Is your dad okay?"

"He's sedated right now, but he came out of the surgery just fine."

The lump grew bigger. I swallowed the dregs of my tea. "I actually haven't heard the news. What kind of surgery did he have?"

"Appendectomy. Pain started up a few days ago, and he ignored it until he turned green in the face and my mom called the ambulance. He'll be fine soon."

I exhaled and glanced at the ceiling. Thank you.

"How long will they keep him? Would he like a visitor?"

"Well, he doesn't even want me to see him in his hospital gown, but if he recovers as planned, he'll be home tomorrow. I'm going back to Davis, but you can call my mom's phone if you want to schedule a visit."

I'd never met Al's wife—she wasn't a church person. Sydney gave me her number, and I scribbled it on the yellow slip. Kayla would have been proud of that organizational stroke of genius, but she was at a dentist appointment so I couldn't brag.

Sydney and I said our goodbyes.

Phew. Al would be okay. What next?

I called Cesar. "How's Phil?"

"He's been asleep for eighteen hours straight and that holding cell is Grand Central."

"Probably still more peaceful than the street. What about the shoes?"

"They match the bloody footprint, and it's too soon for DNA, but the blood type matches Cindy's. It looks like he's our man."

"David, you mean?"

Silence fell across the cell signal connecting us.

Finally, he spoke. "No, Phil. He had the shoes and the cash, Alls."

I bristled to hear my nickname. Wrong time, wrong conversation. "It's too much of a coincidence," I said. "How could he be wearing another suspect's shoes?"

"It's no more of a coincidence than you finding the shoes on a man sleeping in the exact place Cindy died. You aren't the only person who gets all over the neighborhood."

"What about the video footage of David at the BART Plaza? Isn't he wearing the shoes?"

"Resolution isn't high enough to tell. All we can see is black shoes, white soles. He has another pair which match that description—the ones he says he was wearing."

"Maybe David met him on the street, gave him the shoes and the cash."

The sigh crackling in my ear told me Cesar was sick of my interfering before he even spoke. "We have a witness who saw him retrieve the shoes from a grocery bag at the corner of Abbey and Seventeenth on Wednesday evening, before Cindy was murdered."

"What witness?"

Cesar audibly scoffed, like he was clearing phlegm from his throat.

"Let me guess." I listed Phil's cronies in the neighborhood. "Linda? Emile?"

"No and no."

"Rico?"

Cesar hesitated a second too long. "Alma, stay out of it or I will arrest you for interfering in an investigation."

It was a bluff, and we both knew it. He'd look like a fool dragging in his nosy ex. And I knew exactly which bench Rico occupied at Dolores Park.

For good measure, I added, "It's not Phil, Cesar. It has to be David."

"What's your lady friend going to say about that?"

"Don't call her my lady friend. It's demeaning, and I know you're trying to distract me by pissing me off so you can just get off the phone."

That stunned him into silence. If he ever murdered someone, I'd be a shoo-in to solve the case. I could read Cesar like God was whispering truths via the heavenly Wi-Fi.

"Have you arrested him?"

"I'm waiting until he wakes up."

No wonder the kid was sleeping like a fallen redwood.

"What about the murder weapon? Don't you need that to close the case?"

"This isn't TV, Alma. There are always loose ends."

"Since you're so sure it was Phil, tell me what killed Cindy."

"Absolutely not."

Lynn had asked me to keep my eye on Cesar to make sure he did right by Cindy. When I'd agreed, I hadn't for a second believed he'd fail to find the killer. Now, I would have to keep my promise. I would have to talk to Rico.

On my way to Dolores Park, my phone rang. The screen said Naomi. My heart leapt up into my throat, bumping into that lump of emotion that was permanently lodged there.

I was so excited to hear from her I fumbled the phone even though I knew she might say, *Turns out my brother's a murderer.*

Right. There were more important things than a call from the woman who might be my perfect match. I just couldn't think of them at the moment. Inhaling deeply, I waited until my shakes stopped, then pressed the green button. "This is Alma."

"Hey there." I hadn't known it was possible to sound both sultry and cheerful at once. But she did, which left no doubt—Cesar hadn't gotten around to arresting her brother. "Are you free for dinner?"

The moment I'd been waiting for! At least, if I wasn't convinced her brother was the murderer.

"Yeah." Then, because I could hear Kayla griping at me all the way from her dentist's office, I double-checked my calendar. Yep. "I'm free."

I looked up at the ceiling and mouthed, *Thank You.* Time to slam the door on Naomi's winter and put an end to her rainy past, starting tonight.

"Great, because David wants to introduce me to Christina."

My excitement deflated. Double date, or not a date? This sounded more like a friendly David-focused dinner, like our breakfast about the shoes. Oh well. Some relationships got off to a slow start, with friendship coming first. I'm not naturally patient, but I could pretend.

"Wait, we already met Christina, right? She's the one who was trying too hard to look cool and sound dumb?"

"One and the same. But he thinks we didn't get off to a great start."

"Seems like a fair assumption."

"So, they're taking me out to dinner tonight. I don't think I can face this alone. I might pull a full-grown Karen Cohen on him and chew him out for screwing up his marriage and losing his wife and children in front of his mistress."

"Your mom's name is Karen?"

"Yeah." Naomi chuckled. "Glad you're grasping the important details."

She'd already told me those—David wasn't happy with Ms. Allergic to Iguanas, who took their daughter and five-month-old fetus home to her parents.

"What the hell is going to happen to his family if Melissa stays on the East Coast and he opens a bar here? He'll never see his kids. That is not how we were raised."

"Just double checking, do you need moral support, or a buffer, or a referee?

She laughed again, low and throaty. "Not totally sure yet. Can we play that one by ear?"

Gotta love a woman who laughs when she's stressed.

"You realize this sounds like the worst second date ever?" The words flew out of my mouth without bothering to pass through any of my mental filters.

She didn't respond right away, which gave me plenty of time for self-flagellation. Breakfast hadn't really been a date, and I'd already determined to accept her friendship, be patient, play the long game. So why had I blurted out my complaint?

You want to know where you stand, dummy, some internal voice answered.

Then Naomi replied. "It does sound awful. Please come anyway."

Her plea cut straight into me. Plus, there was her sense of humor, her smile, her struggle to move on from a broken heart. All of it persuaded me to accept the invitation, made even more awkward by the fact that I was certain her brother was guilty of murder. Hopefully she'd let me comfort her, once the truth was out.

"We're going to Udupi Garden. I thought it would be good since it's easy to eat vegan there."

My stomach grumbled. Their *dosas* are my favorite. "Perfect. See you there."

Chapter Seventeen

Rico wasn't on his bench. His stuff was there—a handcart crammed full with a sleeping bag and a lumpy stuff sack. I recognized the dingy blue stuffed poodle tied to the side. Plastic shopping bags bulged out between the wire rungs of the cart's sides. Those sorts of bags were scarce since the city banned them years ago. Maybe Rico was a conservationist, reusing them so they didn't end up in the ocean.

I perched on the seat and read a Biblical commentary on my phone, glancing up regularly to scan the grassy slopes. Even on a weekday, the upper terraces of the green space housed a party. Sunbathers spilling out of the Castro to soak up rays in the bowl-shaped park protected from the wind. On a lower level, young children swarmed the playground, parents milling around and chatting while their offspring climbed and slid.

Rico appeared, rounding the corner of the building that housed the older public restrooms—the ones avoided by young families because of the strong likelihood someone would be bathing in the sink or shooting up inside a stall. Sometimes Rico accepted food from me on Sunday nights at the BART Plaza, and I'd seen infected injection sites on his hands. From his languid rolling gait, Rico was high at the moment.

"Hey, Rico. I've been looking for you."

"*Hola, Madré.* What's happening?"

"I'm worried about Phil. The police think he robbed The Carlos Club and murdered the manager."

"Nah. Phil wouldn't hurt nobody. He's gentle. Like Bambi." Rico patted the head of his blue poodle. Did Rico mean the orphaned Disney deer, or had he named his toy after the animated animal? Either way, he was confirming my impression of Phil as harmless as long as you didn't wake him abruptly.

As he arranged the stuffed dog comfortably on the top of his cart, I pulled out my phone, set it to record audio, and inserted it into my pocket. Cesar would be mad at me either way, so I may as well capture Rico's words.

"I think Phil's gentle too. But he was wearing shoes with the victim's blood on them, and you told the police he found them in the trash on Wednesday morning."

"Wednesday?" He scratched his scalp through wooly black hair. "That was a long time back. Can't be sure."

Was Cesar seriously using this guy to corroborate an alibi?

"What day is it today, Rico?"

"Today's Friday, right?" He turned his face up to the warm sun. "I looooove Friday. TGIF."

Not even close, which probably explained why Rico rarely came to the plaza on Sundays to get food. He didn't know what day it was.

"Can you remember where you and Phil were when he found the shoes?"

"Over there, somewhere." He pointed northeast, in the general direction of David's street, on the corner of which Phil had allegedly discovered the Scampers in a trashcan.

"How did he find them?"

"Going through the trash. People throw out good stuff over there. That's where I found Bambi." He patted the poodle.

I couldn't resist. "Why is your dog named after a deer?"

He smacked his forehead like he couldn't believe the idiocy of my question. "Come on, *Madré*. Look at those big, black doe eyes. Poor thing. Left alone in the trash." He stroked the dog's head, and his eyelids drooped.

My chest tightened. "I'm glad he found a good home, Rico. You know what would help Phil? If you can tell me where he got the cash he was carrying?"

"Don't know." Rico shrugged like a kid denying he'd taken candy while his hand was still in the jar.

"Come on, Rico. Wherever it came from, it's not worse than murder, right?"

Rico's eyes went big. "Murder?"

I contained a sigh, trying not to reveal my exasperation that he didn't remember what I'd said two minutes earlier. "The police arrested Phil for murder, because of the bloody shoes and the cash."

"Yeah. Yeah. Right." Rico rubbed his dirty palm over his face. "Okay. I'll spill. But don't tell nobody, okay? Phil's a good kid."

I met Rico's eyes, which he must have taken as an assent.

"You know the Goodwill at Nineteenth?"

I nodded.

"People drop stuff off there when they're closed. Junk, but also nice loot they don't want. And Phil's good with electronics, so he picks through the donations, fixes broken things. Sometimes he scores big, and everybody knows he's the hookup. Last week, he sold three old laptops, an old-school record player, other things too, I guess he was carrying a lot of cash around from his business."

This was the big secret? Hard to believe he could make hundreds of dollars that way. Then again, there was an enormous economic gulf between people buying million-dollar condos and those camping on their sidewalk. Phil's business bridged that gulf. Rich folks' trash was transient folks' treasure. It probably wasn't even illegal if he was going through bags left outside a locked storefront. Had Phil told Cesar this, or was he afraid to admit his scam?

I stood up and extended my hand. "You did your pal a big favor, explaining about his income. Don't worry. He won't get in trouble for his electronics business."

"Good, good. I don't want to be a rat." Rico slumped on his bench, ready for a nap in the sun.

"Have a good day, Rico."

He lifted his fingers from his belly in a farewell wave. I dropped by the family-friendly bathroom to wash my hands, knowing Rico's were covered in sores. I'd pick up a tube of antibiotic ointment for him at the drugstore later.

Then I sent the sound file to Cesar, with a text. *Your shoe timeline is wrong, and Phil didn't rob the bar. He's innocent.*

He didn't reply all afternoon. Probably preferred not to hear me gloat.

Back in my office, I immersed myself in Biblical commentaries and tried to psych myself up for a dinner with the woman of my dreams and her brother who had dumped bloody shoes a block from his apartment after murdering my friend.

Chapter Eighteen

Hours later, I stood at the intersection of Twentieth and Valencia, waiting for the pedestrian signal to cross. A trio I recognized appeared catty corner from me, racing into the street to make it to the opposite side before the countdown hand reached one.

Naomi was out front, David and Christina lagging behind, moving slowly because of her fussy shoes.

Tires squealed.

I rotated my head, searching for the source of the sound. A dark sedan sped into the intersection. It headed straight for David and Christina.

"Move," I shouted.

They hadn't needed my instructions. David spun her, putting himself between his girlfriend and the car while shoving her forward. She ran three steps, then fell. He dragged her up and pulled her clear of the car's tire just in time.

I dashed across the street against the signal and reached Naomi at the same time David and Christina did. The car tore off, leaving the scent of burning rubber in its wake. I squinted to read the license plate, but a dark film covered it. I couldn't make out a single digit. Neither could I identify the make and model of the car. Since I never got a license, I pay little attention.

The four of us stood together, staring after the vehicle. I assumed their hearts were pounding as heavily as mine. Others on the street examined David and Christina as they passed, assuring themselves the pair was unscathed before they continued on their way.

"We were about to be yet another pedestrian hit-and-run."

Christina laughed, reedy and humorless.

I met Naomi's eye. The incident hadn't seemed like a random almost-accident. The car had come from the same direction as they had and pulled out right as David and Christina entered the intersection, and it had deliberately obscured its tag.

"Phew." He pressed his hand to his heart. "I need a drink," he added, a little too lighthearted.

I raked my eyes over him, then Christina. "You're bleeding." She'd scraped her knee, above the top of her black stiletto boots.

David crouched in front of her, drew a handkerchief from his pocket, and pressed it to the wound. She winced and giggled simultaneously.

My mind raced as quickly as the dark car had sped off. Was someone trying to kill David? Why? My mother's cop shows supplied me with a multitude of motives—Had he borrowed money from a crime lord to finance his cocktail bar? Had he stolen Christina from a notorious gangster? What if she was the target? The possibilities were ridiculously sordid for a nice Jewish guy from suburban New Jersey.

A gust of icy wind barreled down the street.

"Ooh. It's freezing out here." Christina shivered, probably as much from shock as a chill. "Let's go inside."

"Go ahead and put our name on the list." Naomi slid me another glance to let me know she wanted to speak to me alone.

David took Christina's elbow and led her through the restaurant door.

As soon as it closed behind them, Naomi spoke. "We have to call the police. That was no accident."

"We should call, although I doubt they'll ever find that car."

She shuddered.

"Go on in. I'll ring the station." I wanted to talk to Cesar without an audience and tell him someone was trying to kill David. Did that mean Naomi's brother was innocent after all? Even if he'd dumped his bloody shoes in the trash near his apartment? It made no sense.

"Thanks." She took a step toward the door, then twisted backward to face me. "Do you think someone wants to kill David, so he takes the fall for the murder?"

"Maybe." This wasn't the time to relish the way our thoughts mirrored each other's.

Behind her tortoiseshell frames her brown eyes darkened, and she nodded before disappearing into the restaurant.

Cesar answered on the first ring.

"Did you get my messages from earlier?"

"I'm taking them into consideration," he said.

I described the near miss car accident. The second I finished my story, he was ready with an answer. "Probably a coincidence. Those near misses happen all the time. We had more than eight hundred pedestrian accidents in the city last year, and for every one of those, there were easily five barely avoided."

"It looked deliberate, Cesar. Like the car was following them."

He paused for a long moment. "Does it strike you as off that it happened in your sight?"

"What do you mean?"

"I mean, coming from Cohen's apartment, they'd walked blocks before reaching that intersection. But the moment they entered your view, a car swooped out."

"You're saying they staged it to convince me David is innocent?" Through the restaurant window, I watched David grin goofily at Christina. It seemed unlikely he would even risk her getting a skinned knee.

"It's a possibility," Cesar said.

"No way." My spine tensed, and outrage gripped me. He wanted to sour me on Naomi, out of jealousy or some dark misanthropic urge. Being a detective had eaten away at his humanity. "You're leaping to wild conclusions, arresting and accusing innocent people left and right. Why don't you do your job and figure out who killed my friend?"

"Believe me, Alma. I'm doing my job. And you need to stay the hell out of it before you get hurt."

"Right. Like I was almost poisoned by medicinal tea?"

"In hindsight, I might have overreacted because, you know..." He cleared his throat. "It's you."

My cheeks heated, and my anger ebbed. He wasn't some misanthrope ruined by his dark profession; he was just worried about me.

I caught sight of Naomi in the restaurant. She watched me, eyebrows raised, then lifted the menu and pointed at it. Time to order.

A man exited the restaurant and the aroma of spices hit me with a blast of warm air. Garlic, ginger and garam masala. My stomach growled.

"Hey, listen, I've got to go."

"Enjoy your dinner."

Silently, I held the phone to my ear trying to decipher his tone. Bitterness, or just a jaded man long ago tired of putting up with my antics.

"Thanks. Take it easy."

"I'll try." And the line went dead.

As I entered the restaurant, I replayed the almost-accident in my mind. I simply couldn't believe David had staged it. But if he wasn't the murderer, and neither was Phil, who did that leave? Back to square one in every murder investigation—the spouse. Could Lynn have fooled me? I shivered, hating the thought that someone I knew could secretly be a killer.

Chapter Nineteen

I entered the restaurant. At David's side, Christina glowed youthfully. Aside from her pink cheeks, she seemed to have recovered from nearly becoming roadkill.

She was at least five years younger than him, perhaps twenty-three to his twenty-eight. She glanced around at others in the restaurant, observing, as if she wasn't sure of the etiquette. Odd, since the Indian place wasn't particularly upscale. She watched a man put his napkin on his lap, then noticed David's was there too and copied the gesture.

Had wolves raised the poor girl on the Canadian tundra?

I waved at Naomi. Everyone at the table stood.

With the imminent danger of the black sedan behind us, I took time to notice Naomi's appearance. She wore a simple black knit dress cinched with a black-and-white beaded belt. It showed off her curvy figure to perfection.

In contrast, Christina's outfit was ridiculous. Those impractical high-heeled boots, a short skirt and flouncy blouse with matching necklace and earrings, and a clutch on the table next to her plate. She was thoroughly over-dressed and over-accessorized for a casual dinner in the Mission. If my pal Suzannah were here, she'd say every item Christina wore vied for the lead, and nothing wanted to play the supporting part.

She extended her hand. "Nice to see you again, Alma. Thanks for your help out there."

If pointing out she was bleeding counted as help, she must not receive a lot of basic human kindness. A possibility that made her etiquette spying and over-the-top outfit take on new meaning.

"I'm glad you're both okay." I shook her hand, then David's.

"And thanks for being a friend to my sister right now, too."

I glanced at Naomi, and color appeared high on her cheeks and across the bridge of her nose.

The sight sent tingles down my spine. "I'm always glad to make a new friend."

She leaned in to hug me and kissed my cheek, whispering. "Thanks for coming. Later, tell me what the detective said."

I nodded, and we took our seats.

The restaurant was loud with conversation and clinking dishes. I leaned across the table toward the couple, not bothering to look at the menu. I always ordered the same *dosa,* a rice pancake smeared with cooked spinach and filled with spiced potatoes. "So, how did you two meet?"

"I started volunteering at the SPCA a few months ago." David sipped from a pilsner glass that contained a golden-colored beer. "It's down the street from the startup where I work, and I really like animals."

Do grown men actually say this, or only guys who want you to think they didn't murder your friend? I tried to imagine the words coming out of Cesar's mouth and had to pinch my nose to contain a snort.

"It's nice to get out of the office for some fresh air and to take a dog on a walk."

Christina's hand moved under the table, presumably to pat his thigh, or possibly to double check on the exact placement of his napkin. "And I've been working there for a year. I want to be a vet, so I'm getting in experience while I finish my prereqs."

"Christina has a degree in PR, but she hated her corporate job." David gazed at her with mooneyes.

She smiled at him. "Just like David."

Naomi made a gagging sound in the back of her throat, but they didn't seem to notice.

Christina tore her gaze off David. "So we began walking dogs together when we could, and we clicked."

"When you're married, you aren't supposed to click with other people." Naomi punctuated her jab with a long sip from a glass of wine.

Damn, the least she could have done was order me one, too.

"Hell, Naomi, we haven't even been here five minutes. You

could at least try to be friendly?"

He had a point, but I admired her directness. Straight to the point was my kind of woman.

Naomi crossed her arms. "Like you tried to work things out with your wife?"

"I did try. We tried for years. Counseling just made it more clear we're incompatible. And that's not Christina's fault."

Naomi stalled, mouth open. She must not have known David and Melissa had been in couple's therapy. Perhaps she didn't know her brother as well as she thought she did.

"You should have considered that before you knocked your wife up with David, Jr." After she lobbed that bomb, she crossed her arms.

Christina's face turned the deep red of shame, not mere embarrassment.

Naomi lowered her gaze. If I was reading her right, she was ashamed, too.

David stood up, the legs of his chair scraping the floor loudly enough to turn heads. "Excuse me. Restroom." He bit out the words through clenched teeth.

Naomi's dark brows tilted into a vee over her glasses.

Christina took a dainty sip of water and leveled Naomi an even stare. "I don't blame you for disliking me."

"I don't dislike you." She sighed. "I just want you to get out of my brother's life so he can fix what he broke and take responsibility for his children."

Damn. Even with David's retreat, we still careened downhill fast, and Naomi hadn't yet told me if I should be the buffer or the referee. I guess that left the decision up to me. With two fingers between my lips, I whistled. Heads turned throughout the restaurant. I held my hands up in a time-out T.

Naomi crossed her arms, slumped in her seat, and guzzled her wine. Whoops. Maybe I should have tried to be a buffer instead. Still, she was beautiful like that, flustered and pink with anger. Would I ever get the chance to kiss that color into her cheeks?

A waiter appeared, and we ordered. He left, and I spied Christina texting under the table. She turned her phone over and leaned closer to Naomi.

"Before David comes back, I need to say something. When we met, it started as a friendship. We talked all the time, and our conversations got deep quickly. I knew he was married, and when I realized how much I looked forward to seeing him, I felt terrible. Like you, I take those vows seriously, and I didn't want to cause any problems. I changed my volunteer schedule to avoid him."

Naomi had been drinking wine with her arms crossed. In deference to the younger woman's confession, she set down her glass and let her hands fall to her lap. I was tempted to mimic Christina's reassuring pat to David's thigh, but I wasn't sure it would be welcome.

"A few weeks later, David showed up on a different day to find me. He'd told Melissa he wanted a divorce, and he hoped to start dating me."

Now Naomi was leaning forward. "When was this?"

"About six months ago. And I said, 'No.' I knew they were unhappy, possibly incompatible, if she was so uncompromising."

Naomi nodded, agreeing with the description of her sister-in-law.

"But if a marriage ends, it shouldn't be over feelings for someone else. That grass is greener stuff is no good."

Okay. So this odd girl, trying too hard to be fashionable and fit in, wasn't so bad after all.

"David went home. We stopped seeing each other at the shelter, stopped texting each other. They tried to work it out. That's when they started counseling. They conceived a baby… "

"Melissa had her IUD removed and didn't tell me until I came home to a 'Surprise! It's-a-Boy!' party one night."

I jerked my head to where David stood. I hadn't noticed him approach. The circles under his eyes contributed to the impression he was ages older than Christina. But if he weren't a murder suspect in the early stages of divorce, expecting an unplanned baby with his estranged wife, they actually made a good match.

Naomi had grabbed the sides of her seat, gripping with white knuckles.

David sat, and the waiter delivered a round of appetizers, including a plate of crispy, hot papadum on the house.

For a moment, things felt so mundanely awkward that I forgot David was my number-one suspect in Cindy's murder. Having successfully refereed the conversation between Naomi and Christina, I buffered with a simple icebreaker.

"So David, what are your favorite bars in the city?"

It sounded friendly enough, but I had an agenda. If he wanted to turn The Carlos Club into Blotto's, where people came from across the bridges to slurp down liter-sized martinis, then pee in the streets, I might need to squeeze Naomi's thigh.

"Well, I like the Orbit Room. That's what I want to do with the Fourteenth Street spot—restore the Victorian details, brighten it up. Have you been to Aldgate West, the gin bar in the Tenderloin?"

"Sure." Cesar's friend Simon had painted the interior, and he got us free drinks every so often. Maybe he could introduce David to the owner if he turned out to be innocent.

"Well I love their menu and their sense of place. I want to create something like that..." He went on, rhapsodizing about his plans. Honestly, it sounded like a great place to live across from.

While he talked, Christina listened, interjecting little comments, reminding him of ideas. He never seemed annoyed at the interruption, but pleased, like she helped him express himself better. If I were doing premarital counseling, that alone would have gotten them a passing grade.

"I'm considering calling it Naomi's."

The Naomi in question squeaked. "What? Why?"

"Well, I didn't set out to evict the only lesbian bar in the city. Calling it David's would only pile on the offense."

"Naming it after your gay sister doesn't earn you extra karma."

"I don't know." I scooted back in my chair to get a better view of her squirming. "It's a great name—timeless, and anybody who knows the Bible knows she's brave, loyal, looks out for other women, and engineers her own happy ending. Way better than calling it Tamar's."

David snorted, earning himself a few points in my book. That Biblical heroine's father-in-law treated her atrociously before she took matters into her own hands.

"Or Bathsheba's." Christina took a sip of water.

Naomi and I turned to her in one synchronized move. A good sign—natural choreography. Once again fulfilling my duty as the referee, I signaled to Naomi that she should speak.

"You know the Bible?"

Christina nodded, glancing a wary look at David. He shrugged.

"I was raised Christian. Very." She mumbled the last word, then shoved a bite of samosa in her mouth.

Naomi glared at her brother. Apparently my refereeing wasn't over. I leaned forward, trying to break the line of laser-hot eye contact between the siblings. "Where did you grow up, Christina?"

"A small town in Idaho." She pulled a wry smile.

Okay, so perhaps the wolves who raised her were from the American tundra.

"And don't worry about stereotyping. It's exactly what you're thinking. Huge family. My parents are total fundies. They live on a compound, think their preacher is a prophet, and forbade me to read books from the library. They cut me off when I came to Cal for college. I paid my way, which is why I chose a career that would compensate me well. I have massive student loans. Sadly, I wound up hating it."

Suddenly her bizarre style and her restaurant manners made more sense. She probably hadn't eaten out much. And once Lily had tried a mail-order fashion styling services where they send you five garments and photos of how to assemble outfits with appropriate shoes and accessories. We'd giggled about the prints-on-prints plus textures galore. Christina looked like she was dressing in the exact outfit she'd seen in a style guide. A Biblical fundamentalist who reads *Glamour* and doesn't trust herself to interpret the suggestions for herself.

I avoid these complicated questions by wearing black, gray and burgundy everything, even underwear. In every combination, they go great with my clerical collar.

"Actually, Christina's upbringing wasn't that different from ours." David dipped some papadum into a red chutney that looked spicy as hell. As soon as it hit his tongue, he coughed.

"We have a big family, too." Naomi completed his thought.

I turned to Naomi. "How many kids are there?"

"Five, including me."

I waited for her to ask Christina, but she didn't, so I did. "How about you, Christina?"

"I'm one of nine. We were super close growing up. Family game nights. Movie nights. Church all day Sunday."

Naomi faced her brother, shaking her head. "Mom is going to kill you."

"Why?" I asked.

Christina stared at me. "She didn't tell you? Number one Cohen family rule: must marry a Jew."

Chapter Twenty

Right. Okay. Should have expected that one.

Warmth bled from my hands. Not like I was dying to get married anytime soon. But I suspected that for Naomi the Cohen family rule probably also meant not making out on my couch, not celebrating each other's religious holidays, not bonding over our hard work pastoring congregations before curling up to eat popcorn and watch *Will & Grace*.

I met her pretty gaze. Her luscious red lips pressed thin and flat, and she nodded.

"But you're Reconstructionist?" A rabbi in the most progressive branch of Judaism. "Why the rule?"

"It's not a rule so much as a family value. Our parents taught us the importance of carrying on our lineage and traditions."

"They go to the Conservative synagogue," David added. "Naomi's already a traitor for turning Reform."

She tilted her head and pouted. "Said the guy leaving his nice Jewish wife for this shiksa."

I recoiled from the word, but Christina just blinked. "Is that an insult?" she asked in a level voice.

"No, honey," David kissed the top of her head. "It means you're especially tempting."

"Is that what it means about me, too?" I turned to Naomi with a mock-hopeful tone, which probably revealed just how betrayed I felt by Christina's revelation. Cesar had been right to warn me off her—she was using me, had known before our almost-kiss I was a priest, even if my half-Asian appearance didn't guarantee my gentile status.

"You have to understand." Naomi squared her shoulders toward me. "On both sides, all our ancestors were decimated in the Holocaust. Both Mom's grandparents were sole, child survivors. They devoted themselves to making a big, joyful, loving family like the ones they'd lost to carry on the traditions. That's important to me, too."

My emotion-goiter swelled up big and fat in my throat, and I wanted to look anywhere other than her apologetic brown eyes. My gaze wandered, landing on David, who wore a pitying expression, then Christina, who's lower lip jutted in solidarity with me. Maybe they would scoot their chairs closer to make room for me on their side of the table.

I know, I know. I should have simply respected her values, her commitment to her culture and her faith. And I did.

Also, I know I must have looked like a complete mess, with my flaking on meetings and my mountain of phone messages—wait, wasn't there somebody I'd forgotten to call back?—But I defied categorization of humans and of paperwork all for the same reason.

When Yeye died, I learned the harm that comes of choosing sides, whether you call it tribalism, ethnic conflict, or identity politics. After the shooting, tensions grew in the neighborhood between the Chinese shop owners and the Latino residents. We only averted a crisis by breaking down our barriers.

I looked between David and Christina, who leaned their shoulders and heads toward each other. Naomi thought he was reckless and irresponsible. But to me they were bold, defying their families' values to be together.

It certainly wasn't easy to imagine this guy, besotted, aspiring bar-owner and animal-lover, bludgeoning Cindy over the head. Even if he had put all his money into opening the bar formerly known as The Carlos Club and felt the strain of his difficult wife taking his daughter and unborn child away.

But if it wasn't David, and it wasn't Phil, who the hell killed Cindy?

I rose and pushed back my chair in one movement, tossing some cash on the table. "Good luck you two." Leveling my gaze at Naomi, I tacked on a, "See you around."

On the way home, I remembered my grandfather's death. For days after Cesar and I found him, I couldn't leave my apartment, haunted by the sight of the black bullet hole through his wizened old forehead.

Cesar came every day. He brought me matcha-flavored soy ice cream, he brought my homework. One day, he told me what was happening outside.

Gang violence had been escalating in the Mission, the boundary between the Mexican-America *Norteño* and *Sureño* gangs contested weekly. The shooting had sparked new tensions. Shop owners, many of whom were Chinese like Dad and Yeye, paid a high price for their strife. Mission High hosted a community meeting. I left the apartment to attend.

The rhetoric got ugly fast. The shop owners announced they were locked and loaded, a sound byte that ran for weeks on the local news. Of course, the Latinos who came to the meeting were parents worried about their kids, small business owners, and laborers. Gangs did not send emissaries to defend their actions. But those hard-working, law abiding Latino folks felt the Chinese had lumped them in with the thugs causing trouble and sensed the sharp mistrust when they shopped for produce at markets like Lee's Grocery.

After the meetings, street fights broke out in the neighborhood, and the tensions barged their way into my school.

People couldn't tell where I fit by looking at me. Was I Chinese or Latina? Sometimes they assumed I had a lot of *Indio* blood. But when they learned my name, they often figured it out.

I played the chameleon, hung with both groups at school. Spoke both my mother tongues. The truth was, I was wholly and completely both, like Jesus is human and divine. I spoke Cantonese and Spanish, could cook both cuisines. I had aunties and *tias* all over the Mission, two different kinds of brown. So it hurt to see the kids going at each other as if Latinos and Chinese are natural enemies.

They very fact of my existence and my parents' happy marriage means that can't be true. When my mom, pregnant at 25, quit City College to marry my dad, who helped his father run Lee's Grocery on the corner of 19th and Mission, neither set of my grandparents was thrilled. But everyone quickly saw how much they loved each other, how good they were together.

I took it as a personal affront that my two communities were attacking each other because of the actions of one murderer and a bunch of kids who had fallen astray. I spoke up about it at school, and people listened. In English class, we had heated discussions that spilled onto the lunch yard. Those conversations continued onto the sidewalk, the corner stores and parks, and home with the students. We were fired up, outraged, and then I proposed a walkout. The message spread with text messages and chat apps.

The second Monday of October, fifteen minutes into first period, every kid at Mission High walked out of class. We'd stashed signs and banners in our lockers. Some teachers had gotten wind of the plan and left with us in support and to keep their eye on things. Our posters read, *One Mission*, or *Stop the Violence,* or *Peace* in all the language spoken by kids in our school.

When folks passed by me with my *Love* poster, they high-fived me. "Nice job, Alma." People gave me credit for the whole thing, and although it had taken many kids and teachers getting on board—they were right—I'd been the one to stir and spark, talk and teach, until it took off. That's the day I became an activist, by refusing to be one thing, by defying binary categories, by embracing the glorious fluidity of life.

The gang violence didn't stop, but the neighborhood united against it, and that was much better than turning on each other.

These ideals didn't necessarily have to manifest on my desk as administrative chaos, but that's the way I approached things— open, always ready to be surprised, to be led, to learn and grow.

Still, I knew the Bible well enough to sympathize with Naomi's family values. The Jews had been threatened with annihilation repeatedly throughout their history. I understood wanting to preserve her traditions rather than toss them in a melting pot with all of mine. What I didn't understand was why she hadn't told me herself before tonight. Was Cesar right that she'd been stringing me along in case I could help her brother?

What a fool I'd been. Shame tightened my scalp and my head hurt. Time to let go of the fantasy of helping her finally find her springtime.

I arrived home with no memory of walking down Valencia Street. Stupid—I should have been paying more attention if I didn't want to be pedestrian collision number 801.

After brushing and flossing, I went straight to bed.

Chapter Twenty-One

When my alarm woke me for the sprint to Morning Prayer, I sat up straight, my heart pounding.

I showered, dressed, and dashed to the church with my tea in hand. With Al sick, we numbered only three.

After the service ended, Jenny approached me with sympathy in her eyes. "I visited Al yesterday."

"That's great. I thought he wasn't coming home until today."

"He's not. I went to the hospital."

Okay. So apparently the daughter hadn't warned Jenny about his preference not to be seen in his hospital gown. "How's he doing?"

"He says he's OK, but I'm not convinced. His wife thinks he needs to step down from the bishop's committee, and I agree."

Wait. Had I missed something? "Appendectomies are rough, but healthy people recover from them pretty quickly."

"She says he's not as well as he claims, and I got the feeling they've been keeping his health concerns private. I know how busy you've been, helping the police investigate Cindy's murder, and I didn't want to worry you over it. But I ran into the bishop at the Hillside Supper Club last night, so I brought him up to speed on everything and offered to step in as senior warden."

"Oh?" Apparently, becoming a supervisor or a bishop got you invited to one of the most exclusive private clubs in the city. I thought only the likes of Kevin Kearney dined there. Belatedly, I remembered I owed the bishop a phone call. Of all the yellow slips of paper to misplace.

"I hope you don't mind us deciding without you, but I know

how much you have on your mind."

"Sure. If that's what Al wants."

The sympathetic look in her eye hadn't faded, like she was holding another shoe aloft, waiting for the invitation to drop it.

"Is there something else?"

"You should know I've spoken to a few other members of the committee. I'm sorry to say, Al isn't the only one concerned about your focus. You know I'm one hundred percent in your camp, but everyone else has a story or two about your missed appointments, your perpetual absence from the office... There is a general sense you're failing to prioritize, Alma."

Her words hit me hard and quick, right in my Achilles heel, raw from Kayla's nagging. Had Jenny been spying on me at my newly clean desk? Or did everyone in my church secretly think I was a scatterbrain?

"It's this murder. It's shaken me up. And there's so much to do—"

"Alma. The police have a lot to do. But your job is to pastor St. Giles'. Not play Watson to Detective Garza."

Well, she had that analogy backwards. I'd found the shoes, exonerated Phil, eliminated Kearney as a suspect. Clearly, I was Holmes in our partnership. The problem was, Cesar never had liked playing sidekick.

She sighed and put her hand on my shoulder. "Alma, I know Cindy was a friend—she was mine, too. But as leaders, we always face extenuating circumstances, trying to draw our focus away from our mandates. You are the priest-in-charge of St. Giles'. You want to be our rector, and I'm confident you can do it. But don't give your detractors any more to complain about, okay?"

I clasped my hands behind me so she wouldn't see how they shook. It's important for leaders to hear criticism non-defensively, and I was lucky to have someone with so much experience to mentor me.

"Thanks, Jenny."

She opened her arms, and I stepped in, accepting her hug.

A few moments later, I sat at my desk. Was she right? Had I lost sight of my job over the last few days? Days—an important word, for the sake of scale. Even if I'd been distracted from my work, less than a week had passed. A head cold could keep me out for that long.

Or was this a bigger problem? Perhaps my vision didn't match up with the people of St. Giles? Perhaps I wasn't transparent enough about how I spent my time?

My mind raced, searching for evidence of either possibility, brainstorming tactics to fix both problems. A glance at my computer screen revealed I'd been sitting there thinking for almost half an hour with nothing to show for it.

Damn. Thinking about a problem head-on at my desk never solved anything. I either needed to take a walk or let my mind process that dilemma in the background while I ticked off some boxes on the to-do list. Not that I usually made them. Playing whack-a-mole with the small brush fires the Holy Spirit set around me was so much more fun.

Oh, well. To everything there is a season, and a time to every purpose under heaven: A time to be born, and a time to die; a time to sew, and a time to reap; and a time to set priorities and a time to make to-do lists. I surveyed my neatly labeled trays of papers. Where to start?

I dropped onto the floor and found the missing yellow slip. "Call Bishop Vasquez."

No time like the present. I picked up the handset.

Next to it on my desk, my cell phone rang. The screen read Naomi.

I didn't answer. Maybe I was being stupid—it's not as if she'd promised me anything. We'd never even kissed. Eventually, the sense of betrayal would fade and I'd be ready to be friends, but at the moment Cesar's warnings about her felt keenly accurate.

A text message flashed on the screen. *Please pick up. It's about David.*

Seconds later, the phone rang again.

"Hello?"

"They arrested him." She sobbed into the phone.

I'd expected it for days. But after dinner with him, the news crashed down on me. No way could he be the murderer.

"Where are you?"

She sniffed. "I'm at work. Christina was with him when the police came. She called me."

How sisterly. "Do you want me to come there?"

"No. I want you to go to the police station and talk to your detective friend."

There it was. Final confirmation she'd been using me. But, of course, I would go. Not just for her, but for David, and most of all because Cindy deserved justice.

"All right." I ended the call, stood, and shrugged into my leather jacket.

Well, one bit of good news—I didn't have to figure out which pile on my clean desk to start with. I'd just have to call the bishop later.

I dashed out and past Kayla's desk, running straight for the door to Fourteenth Street. With one foot on the sidewalk, I halted and backtracked until I stood right in front of her.

"I'm going to the police station. There's news on Cindy's murder."

Kayla smiled brightly. "Thank you for telling me."

Now, if I could just figure out how to make a to-do list, the new-and-organized Alma might prove a success.

I was breathing heavy by the time I reach the police station. Mario saw me enter through the glass window and waved me back to the workspace. Caesar was bent over his desk.

"Hey, Alma." Mario raised his fist for a bump. Once upon a time, the gesture had been the start to an elaborate secret handshake. Today, we just let our fists fall to our sides.

Cesar closed his laptop. "I was about to call you."

"You're not going to arrest me for interviewing Rico?"

He shook his head. "I expected you to, once you threatened me. A beat cop called me when she saw you there."

I curled my fingers into fists. I hate being predictable.

"If you were determined to meddle, it was a harmless direction. I already knew those two have no idea what day it is, or if it's six in the morning or 6 p.m."

"So you already knew Phil didn't get the shoes before the murder and kill Cindy while wearing them?"

"Yep." A twitch of Cesar's cheek showed his effort not to look smug.

"How?"

"Video footage we got off one of the neighbor's houses. A security camera mounted over the door." Cesar slid a photo across his desk. It showed David walking down Abbey Street sock footed, not a shoe to be found in the image. The time signature read 12:36 AM. He'd dumped his shoes between the BART Station and

135

walked home after leaving The Carlos Club for the second time.

The lie made him look guilty as hell. Could I have been wrong about him? Were we really all capable of murder, even guys who love kitten?

But he loved awkward, trying-too-hard Christina, too... No. He couldn't have smashed Cindy's head in. There had to be another explanation.

"Can I talk to him?"

Cesar spluttered. "Absolutely not."

"Then tell me what he says. Why was he out in his socks? Where the hell did his shoes go in those five blocks between the BART Plaza and his flat?"

"He's got his lawyer with him, and they've changed his story completely. Now he admits he went there, found her dead, and knew he'd be the prime suspect after their argument. So he tried to cover up his presence there."

"That's plausible."

"Yeah, except who killed her between the end of the party and David showing up half an hour later?" Cesar turned up his palms. "When people get caught in a lie like this, they always have a back-up story. But my money's on him."

"What about the attempted hit and run? What if it was the real murderer trying to shut him up, so he'd take the fall."

"Maybes are not evidence."

"And the murder weapon? It's real evidence. You can't close a case without that."

"Yes, actually, I can. But wait--what if the bottle's turned up on the doorstep of your church?" His smile mocked me. "Quick, hurry back to St. Giles' and see if it's there right now."

I poked his sternum. "Be nice." My chest ached for Naomi and her brother. "What happens next?"

"We're questioning him now. We'll charge him soon. I'm certain David Cohen is our guy."

"What kind of liquor bottle was it? Square? Round? A liter? A fifth?"

"Alma, give it up. Trying to find a liquor bottle in forty-nine square miles of city is less likely than a needle in a haystack." Cesar shook his head.

I seemed to inspire the gesture so often he would need a neck massage if this case dragged on much longer. It was hard to be sure after 13 months, but I don't think it was like that when we were together.

"Just tell me. What harm can it do?"

"You can tell someone else and screw up my case."

"Come on. I keep secrets for a living. Want me to run back and get my stole?"

"No."

I made the sign of the cross, which had zero relevance in the situation. Maybe he'd think of it as crossing my heart.

"It was a liter, square bottle."

"Like Jack Daniels?"

"Yeah, although we can't be sure of the label."

As soon as I'd formed the picture in my mind, I saw his point. Sweet baby Jesus. A single liquor bottle would be impossible to find in the city. It had surely gone to the recycling center, along with any fingerprints it bore.

Which it probably did because the attack on Cindy had been a crime of passion.

Caesar was right. The murder weapon wasn't going to get David off the hook. I'd have to find another way.

In the bright light outside, I remembered Naomi wasn't at David's but at work. Like I should be, according to the members of my bishop's committee, who would soon decide whether or not to hire me permanently.

Too bad I'd involved myself in a murder investigation. But that was a conversation to have with the bishop just as soon as I'd checked on Naomi, wracked my brain to figure out who the real murderer was, and ideally found a liquor bottle in a haystack.

I hoofed it over to Congregation Tikkun Olam, just up Dolores from David's apartment. The day was turning warmer, but a breeze rustled the fronds of the palm trees along the median.

The synagogue's arts-and-crafts style building had a fresh coat of sea-green paint with butter-yellow trim. I rang the doorbell and was buzzed in.

The receptionist wore a sleek black bob with one thick silvery streak at her temple. She lowered her red reading glasses. "Can I help you?"

"I'm here to see Naomi Cohen."

She nodded vigorously, her worried gaze darting down a hallway. "She's in a meeting."

Wow. Color me impressed. She somehow managed to focus on her work while I focused on her problems. Not that I could blame her for my professional flaws.

I glanced around the office. It resembled St. Giles's space and every other church front office I'd ever been in, complete with white board, large wall calendar, and a well-thumbed congregational directory open on the desk. Potted plants thrived in four corners, making for excellent *feng shue* and reminding me of Cindy's wilting philodendron.

"I'll wait. She's expecting me."

"Of course." She waved toward a seating area.

As soon as I sat, two emails arrived almost simultaneously, buzzing on my phone.

"Would you like tea?"

I'd left my cup on my desk and wanted another like a junky needs a fix, but I had no desire to put the woman out in addition to invading her workspace. "No thanks."

One upside to being a scatterbrain is that my mind processes a lot in the background. I wake up with sermons ready to preach. I think of solutions to problems in the midst of conversations about entirely different problems. Sadly, I have no control over the process, but I've learned to trust it.

Why not assign my brain a specific task? *Who else would have wanted Cindy dead? And could that liquor bottle be anywhere besides the sorting center in Brisbane?*

In the peace and quiet of the Congregation Tikkun Olam office, I replied to a backlog of emails, then dropped by the St. Giles' Facebook group to do digital pastoral care.

"Sounds great." Naomi's voice came from down the hall sounding steady but strained. "I'll look forward to your email."

I stood as she emerged with a middle-aged man.

"Hi." She sagged when she saw me, as if she was no longer obligated to hold herself up. "Give me a second."

"Sure."

Turning back to the man, she extended her hand. "I'm so glad we could put these plans in place."

"Me, too." He did the double clasp, encasing her hands between his palms. He wore a ponytail, hoop earrings, and a few extra pounds around his middle.

All right buddy. That handshake is lingering too long. Naomi needed a girlfriend to cue the grabby dudes to respect her personal space. A nice, Jewish girlfriend with whom to breed a nice, big Jewish family.

Mr. Grabby smiled wistfully as he passed me, as if he knew neither one of us stood a chance with Naomi of the intelligent eyes and sinfully sexy lips.

She glanced at the receptionist. "Sylvia, I'll just chat with Alma quickly before our meeting."

"No problem. Take your time." Sylvia opened her eyes wide, pleading, like she hoped I could perform miracles that might help Naomi.

Did she know the one where an earthquake breaks open Paul's jail cell? Probably not since it was in the Acts of the Apostles, not part of the Hebrew Scriptures. The best she might hope for was David Cohen surviving a fiery furnace or a lion's den.

Naomi's office had bare walls in need of a coat of paint and a tower of unpacked moving boxes. Her desk was neither a cyclone of papers nor a tidy array of piles. She'd crammed it full of tchotchkes—figurines, stones and crystals, decorative tiles.

Huh. I'd have pegged her for a mountain-of-paper girl like me.

She flung herself into an armchair on the visitor's side of her desk. "What happened at the station?"

I took the adjacent chair. "They have evidence that your brother left the flat on Wednesday night. Security cameras and a bloody shoe print show he was at the murder scene at approximately the time of the murder."

A sound emerged from her throat, halfway between a wail and a whimper.

"It gets worse. They have video of him walking home barefoot after he dumped the shoes. It doesn't look good for him."

"No. He wouldn't do it. He couldn't do it." She closed her eyes, face pointed toward the ceiling.

"I believe you. I didn't until last night. But I do now."

She turned to me, opening her eyes. They shone with gratitude and… Was that something more?

She licked her lower lip with the pink tip of her tongue, and my belly tingled.

Sweet baby Jesus, Alma, you are such a sucker.

"I just wish I knew who it could've been." In the ten minutes since I'd tasked my brain with computing this answer, I'd gotten exactly zero bright ideas. Sometimes it took weeks. The wind blows where it will, and all that.

"Yeah." Her voice shook on the single syllable.

"I'm not giving up, Naomi. I'll figure this out."

"Thanks." Her hollow tone utterly lacked hope.

Voices sounded in the hall, followed by a peel of laughter.

She rose and grabbed my hand from the arm of the chair. "Let's get out of here. Where can we go for some privacy?"

"My place?" I felt my brows lift and tried not to let any undue hopes rise with them.

"Perfect." She pulled those gorgeous lips of hers into a grateful smile.

I followed her out of the office like a sheep behind its shepherdess.

Chapter Twenty-Two

When we got to my place, Naomi swiveled her head, wide-eyed. "Wow."

"What?"

"It's so clean."

This revelation might come as a surprise, given the state of my office. But that is the domain of my mind, my obligations, my chaotic thought processes. The cottage is tidy thanks to my minimalist philosophy. I don't have a lot of clothes or much furniture. And I have absolutely no tchotchkes.

"Did you just move in here?" asked the wrong woman.

"Nope. I prefer to keep things simple." Cesar would have laughed at that, well aware of how little time I spent in my refuge. But Naomi didn't know better.

"So I see." She ran her hand over the velvet upholstery of my sofa—a housewarming gift from my parents and altogether too high-end for my budget. "Hey, can I give my mom a call? David and I haven't been completely honest with her about… all this." She tilted her head toward The Carlos Club, outside and across the street. "It's time to tell the truth."

"Sure. Use my bedroom. I'll find us something to eat."

In the kitchen I scrounged for comfort food. It seemed way too early for microwave popcorn. Voila! A box of graham crackers appeared from behind my bag of quinoa. And I had a jar of peanut butter in the fridge.

I was in the middle of slicing apples in the galley kitchen when Naomi reappeared, her eyes red and puffy.

"All right?"

She nodded, though clearly she wasn't.

"My mom is furious at me for keeping this from her. And of course, David is blameless because accusing him of something else on top of murder would be..." She shrugged. "I don't know. Disloyal?"

"I'm sorry."

"She feels powerless, and she's not good at accepting that, so she spins in a vortex of angry panic. She did it when I got dumped and was still freaking out about Melissa leaving David until this came along. I can see she's only making her stress worse, but I kind of feel the same way—like I want to scream and cry because there's nothing I can do to help."

I experienced that sensation at least once a day, walking through my neighborhood, visiting someone at the hospital, watching the news. No good strategy became clear until I'd let the angry panic ebb.

I set down the knife and stepped toward her. "OK, don't judge me for this, but my pastoral care often involves binge watching episodes of *Will & Grace* until someone feels good enough to talk or plan."

"Judge you? That's genius! Why didn't they teach me that in rabbinical school?"

Oh, this woman. If I believed in a judgmental God, surely Naomi had been sent to punish me for some terrible sin. She was so perfect and yet so out of reach.

"Wait, is it possible just to mainline *Will & Grace*?" She rolled up her sleeve to expose the thin, soft skin of her inner elbow and her bracelet, which still struck me as sad, not hopeful. "I have a good vein right here."

"I don't think technology has come quite that far."

She'd sought me out for comfort, but that didn't mean I was the one to end her winter. She needed a friend. I served the peanut butter, graham crackers, and apples on an enamel tray that my grandmother had brought from China. Naomi's eyes widened and teared up.

Crap. Was she allergic to peanuts?

She sniffed. "My grandma always made me this when I was a kid."

I tucked her in under my throw, turned the TV on, and placed a peanut butter and cracker sandwich in her hand. As soon as the opening credits played, my brain began to make progress on the problem. I needed something to write on, and I hadn't checked in with Kayla in two hours, which violated our new agreement.

"I'm going to run over to the office for just a second. I won't be gone five minutes."

"No problem."

I rushed through the front office and to my desk.

"Everything OK at the police station?" Kayla called out from her chair as I rummaged for a note pad and pencil. Thankfully, she hadn't imposed her tyranny on the contents of my drawers yet.

Ah ha! I found a notepad from the Church Pension Fund, shoved it in my pocket, then presented myself before her. "They arrested somebody, but it's not the right guy." It hit me all at once—Naomi vegging on my couch, David in an interview room or a cell somewhere. My throat tightened, and I could hardly breathe.

She frowned. "How do you know it's the wrong guy?"

"Just do."

She put her forehead in her palm. "You have to let the police do their job. You can't go around second guessing them."

I left before she could spit out a lecture about my lack of focus.

Back in the cottage, Naomi hadn't moved a millimeter. I settled in beside her on the couch and doodled on the paper while she watched TV.

After the detours of suspecting Lynn and Phil, I found myself back at square one: Who wanted to stop Cindy from staying in The Carlos Club besides David and Kevin Kearney?

And me. I'd wanted her to quit her fighting enough to storm out of her big party.

Naomi shifted closer, bringing our thighs into contact on the couch. The warmth of her next to me calmed my breathing.

Maybe someone else at the party had grown tired of Cindy's schemes. Maybe they'd argued... But who?

Naomi wriggled, drawing even nearer.

I inched my elbow toward my waist to make room for her and found myself sketching a square shaped liquor bottle.

Damn, Naomi smelled good. Was it her shampoo? Or some perfume?

I drew the spiraled ridges where the screw cap lodged.

Where could it be? If the recycling truck picked up a bottle at a

143

residence, it went straight to the sorting center in Brisbane. But on the night before pickup, folks roamed the streets collecting bottles and cans to redeem them for their five-cent deposits.

The South Mission recycle center was open tomorrow. If someone from the neighborhood had grabbed the murder weapon from a bin, it might end up there.

But what an *if*. People came from every neighborhood in the city to rifle through the bins. Any of the city's centers could have accepted it in exchange for the five-cent deposit on the bottle.

Still, I should mention it to Cesar.

"What are you drawing?"

I turned toward Naomi and found her face very close to mine.

"Nothing." I flipped over the note pad.

Her eyes searched my face. "I'm sorry I didn't tell you about the Cohen family rule."

"That would have been nice."

"I felt like if I told you, I'd have to stop spending time with you. And you're fun, and funny, and we get each other." She took off her glasses and set them on the arm of the sofa.

Well, at least I'd been reading her signals right all along. "Now I know the rule, and I'm still around."

"Are you?" Her gaze fell to my lips.

"Yep." I said, even though what she was asking didn't seem at all simple.

"Good." She leaned forward and finally, days since we were this close the first time, she kissed me.

Her soft lips on mine stole my thoughts. No wonder people were always having sex in dire situations in books and movies—it had a way of distracting you from your problems.

Somehow she ended up on top of me. And sweet baby Jesus, thank you for bras that hook in front, for permission to touch parts of Naomi even softer than her lips.

Her thigh rubbed between mine, rubbed me in ways no one had in a while. Heavy breaths had stolen our words for a long stretch when she put my hands on the fly of her slacks.

Damn, I wanted what she was offering. I bit my tongue and took deep breaths.

"I think we should stop."

"I don't want to." She reached for the button on my jeans, her fingertips on my belly sending a shower of sparks through me.

I stilled her hand. "Neither do I, but we should. Things will get messy if we keep going."

She brought my palm up to her soft, full breast and kissed me again. This time, I didn't kiss her back.

"Right." She sat up and turned away from me to refasten her bra, her eyes low. "Sorry. That wasn't fair."

"I'm not worried about fair. I just don't want to be that shiksa you hook up with sometimes."

She winced. "I hate that word, and I shouldn't have said it to Christina, but I take your point." She stood and straightened her clothes. "I should go."

"You don't have to go."

"I do, it's cowardly to hide out here searching for distractions. I'm going to call David's lawyer, and then I'll try to go back to work."

"Right." A different kind of distraction, at her office instead of on my couch, one that was probably better for both of us.

At the door, she gave me a stiff hug.

"Call me." I squeezed her waist, wanting to draw out her awkwardness, throw it away, restore the possibility of friendship.

"Yeah." She didn't meet my gaze again before she walked away.

Well, crap. That hadn't ended well.

I dropped back onto my couch and stared at the bottle I'd drawn on my notepad. Tomorrow morning, all the neighborhood's recycling would collectors would redeem their bottles and cans.

Would the murder weapon be among them?

Chapter Twenty-Three

I laced up my boots and hustled to the police station without telling Kayla I'd left the premises.

At the reception desk, I asked for Cesar.

An officer showed me into a room I'd only glimpsed on my earlier visits. The one with the murder board. Cesar stood before it, removing the items taped to its surface.

I stepped through the door. "What are you doing?"

He turned and swept his gaze over me. Could he tell I'd come straight from a make-out session cut short? If I could read his eye movements to know when he was lying, it seemed likely he sensed my disappointment.

Showing me his back, he removed another photo. "We charged David Cohen with the murder. The case is closed."

"Shit."

"Sorry if that's inconvenient to your love life."

I took a deep breath. This was too important to let him bait me. I wondered if I should call Naomi? What would I say since she'd just left my place half an hour ago, trembling and with her lower lip swollen from kisses?

In the absence of a scathing retort, Cesar did a double take. "You okay?"

How did I look? Like someone dumb enough to fall for a woman who'd been clear a relationship with me wasn't on the table? I'd known her less than a week. It couldn't be half as bad as I'd looked when he'd left me. But he'd vanished from my life entirely and never seen how ugly things had gotten for me in the weeks that followed.

"Yeah. I'm fine." I studied the pictures remaining on the board.

"Uh uh." He wagged his finger and sidestepped to block the photos from my view.

"What does it matter now? You've got your man."

"Fine." He punctuated his resignation with a sigh and moved to clear my view.

In the top right corner of the board hung a cluster of photos showing a pool of blood on the concrete floor of The Carlos Club. Cindy's blood, and so much of it.

The breath flew out of me, and I had to grip the edge of the board to stay upright.

Cesar watched, but didn't offer me a hand.

Someone had circled one of the photos with blue dry-erase marker. It featured a shoe print, the perfect match to the sole I'd found Phil wearing.

There was a sketch of a liquor bottle too, one that looked remarkably like mine.

A snapshot of the keys hung there, the red-tagged master from Kearney properties.

Beneath it, another photo. What was it? I leaned in closer. A small blue circle glinted with the camera flash on the concrete floor, near the pool of blood.

"Is this a sequin?" I pointed.

"Yeah. We found it at the scene, but it's probably nothing."

I tried to remember the crowd. Had I seen anyone wearing sequins? Chelle had sported that tank top with the sequined rainbow applique. She was certainly capable of swinging a liquor bottle hard enough to smash Cindy's skull. But what motive did she have?

And Cesar was right. It might have come off any of the patrons that night, or all week, for that matter, given the generally unswept status of the floors.

"Listen, Cesar I have an idea. Tomorrow morning, every recycling collector in the Mission will be in the Savesmart parking lot redeeming their bottles and cans for deposits. Hopefully, the murder weapon will be among them."

"That's an epic long shot, Alma."

"Can you send your officers to go through the bottles?"

A laugh burst from Cesar—deep, low and so genuine that it didn't even mock me. He just thought the idea was completely absurd.

"Don't laugh. It's a good idea."

"Alma, we closed the case. There's no way the captain would authorize me to send even one officer to search through the garbage. We have enough evidence to convict."

"As if getting a conviction has anything to do with finding the guilty person."

His fingers curled around a photo, bending it. He turned back to the board. "Don't start with me, Alls."

"Come on, miscarriage of justice happens all the time. Especially in murders.

"Alma, do not screw with me, or my case, anymore. I've patiently tolerated your personal interest, but you're not even an amateur detective. I saw you go white when you looked at these." He pointed at the pool of blood, shiny and dark, that had once been inside my friend. Blood that might still bring her brain oxygen if I hadn't left her at the bar that night.

The lump in my throat swelled. "Cesar, he didn't do it."

"You believe no one you know personally could kill someone. But I have seen perfectly human, perfectly decent people with blood on their hands too many times to count."

I thought of the boy who'd killed Yeye, scarcely older than I'd been at the time. "I'm aware of that. I'm not a Pollyanna. People get trapped. They get scared."

"And sometimes they get plain old mad. This is the scene of an angry, angry murder."

The lump swelled even larger in my throat. I tried to swallow.

Somehow, Cesar's eyes darkened and shone at the same time. He took a step closer, swept his gaze over the length of me. "And believe me, I know you're not a Pollyanna."

Heat flared in my body. It didn't help that I'd let Naomi stoke it so high before I'd stopped her. I blew out a breath. Surprisingly, it didn't blister the whiteboard or curl the edges of the remaining photos with its blazing temperature.

"And I know you're a good cop. You don't want someone innocent to go down for murder."

A murmur sounded behind me. A group of officers gathered outside the murder room. Had we been loud enough to draw a crowd?

Mario stepped inside. "You guys OK?

"Alma was just leaving," Cesar growled. "Can you show her out?"

"Sure thing."

Even though he was wrong. Even though he didn't trust my intuition and was willing to stack up his evidence against an innocent man, I didn't want to leave. Next to him, I was doing something.

If I headed back to my office, I'd have a clean desk full of work, and not a damn clue how to help David.

Still, I let Mario take my elbow and guide me out of the station. The whispers and murmurs followed us.

Captain Tang came to stand in a doorway. As his gaze followed me out, he nodded and spoke into his phone, although he was too far away for me to hear his words.

I whispered to Mario. "I'm bad for Cesar's reputation, aren't I?"

"There might be speculation he's letting you meddle because he's still…"

"Pussy whipped?"

Mario coughed. "Something like that."

Was he still hung up on me? The possibility worked space into my spine so I felt quite a bit taller than the five feet I measured.

"Thanks for telling me." I hugged Mario. "I'll try to limit my criticisms to when we're in private."

"Are you planning to be in private with him much?"

I shrugged. "You know me. I never plan more than fifteen minutes ahead."

"Double booked for your own funeral is what Cesar used to say." Mario's eyes knew too much over his sad smile.

It seemed like he was waiting for reassurance I wouldn't hurt his brother again. As if I'd done the hurting in the first place. I didn't bother to put Mario at ease. There was no point. Cesar and I both knew better than to get involved again. Nothing had changed.

I saluted Mario, who entered the station, leaving me alone on the sidewalk. As if Cesar had been reading my mind, he sent me a text. *Now that the case is closed, it's best if we stop bumping in to each other.*

He was right, as right as he'd been to dump me in the first place, as right as I'd been to stop things with Naomi at second base. Why did *right* often hurt as much as *wrong*? And *wrong* was always so much more fun.

Kayla called. Thank God. It was like having one of the papers on my tidy desk leap up and volunteer, *Me first!*

"Hey. What's up?"

"Where are you?" she whispered.

"Sorry, sorry. I shouldn't have left without telling you. I'm on—"

"No. I don't care about that—at—at."

"Why's there echo on you end?"

"I'm in the bathroom. Tish Trescott is out there, and she's rummaging through the treasurer's files. She wants copies of all the financial statements since your start date."

My stomach sank. Not that I had anything to hide in the financial statements. Jenny had said members of the bishop's committee had concerns about my performance, but I hadn't imagined Tish—treasurer and Morning Prayer regular—among them. If my closest allies were turning against me, I'd failed badly.

"Give her a copy of whatever she wants. The records are public and she won't find anything incriminating in there."

"She's on the phone with someone, and she said something about money given to the Save The Carlos Club fundraising site. You didn't…?"

"I gave a hundred dollars from my discretionary account when the site first went up, and I'm allowed to give that money to charitable causes at my discretion. Hence the name."

"Okay. Good. Are you on the way back here? Because she made a comment about you being at the police station instead of the office, and… I don't want them to have anything else to hold against you."

Right.

"How did she know I was there?" Even Kayla hadn't known.

"Does she know somebody at the station?"

It wasn't impossible. Tish wasn't a native, but she'd lived in the city since college and had kept the books for lots of local nonprofits in that decade.

Something crashed on Kayla's end of the phone.

"What was that?"

Kayla exhaled. "On second thought, you should stay out of here until she leaves. I'll call you when she's gone."

"Great. Thanks."

I crossed the street in front of Good Vibrations—yes, the city's best sex shop is across the street from the Mission Police Station. San Francisco—it's a helluva town.

Between my shoulder blades, my muscles pulled tight. Tish checking the church finances felt like a betrayal. Then again, Naomi had left me raw and inclined to the feeling. It was a treasurer's job to be sure the expenditures were appropriate and in-line with the budget, and I'm not exactly known for my attention to details.

I phoned Jenny. The call went to voicemail. I didn't leave a message. Moments later, my device buzzed with a text. *In a meeting. Can't talk. Don't worry about Tish. Al stirred everyone up, but I will calm the waters. I'm on your side.*

I exhaled a shaky breath and scanned the intersection. The scene looked especially crisp and bright—-the lines of the buildings and windows were sharp, the green leaves and colorful clothing of pedestrians vibrant. Kayla's phone call must have shot me through with adrenaline.

Often, I walk through the neighborhood when I need to think through my sermon or dream up a great tactic for a community project. Exiled from the office, a stroll was my best option. I pulled up the lessons assigned for Sunday on my phone, read through them, and took off south on Valencia.

Savory aromas filled the street from the cafes. The grilled cheese shop occasionally made me lust for a serving of dairy, and today was no different. Bike messengers zoomed past. Cars honked when they got stuck behind someone double-parked. High-end furniture shops and clothing boutiques had replaced the dollar stores and thrift shops of my youth.

I missed the grungier, more diverse vibe, but I still loved the vibrancy—the cafes, the coffee shops, the gourmet chocolatier who made several vegan bars and truffles upon which I occasionally splurged.

At twenty-fourth I turned off the main drag and walked back up Capp, a residential street with some gentrified blocks and some stubbornly holding on to the older, down-home days of the Mission. As I approached Eighteenth, someone had already dragged out their garbage bins. Kim, one of the long-time collectors, rifled through the big blue one.

"Hey Kim, how's it going?"

He stood up and shielded his eyes from the sun to see me. "Hey,

Rev! Good to see you. How are your parents?"

"They're OK, thanks. Hey, I have a question. I'm looking for a bottle with a square shaped body, about this big." I held up my hands. "Probably thrown out last Wednesday night or Thursday morning."

Kim chuckled. "A bottle, you say? Seen a few of those."

"Yep. Practically impossible, right? But this bottle is really important. If I could find it, it would change someone's life."

Kim scratched his salt-and-cinnamon beard and winked. "Does it have a message in it? Or a genie?"

"Neither, but could you put the word out in the neighborhood that I need it? I'll be at the collection tomorrow morning down at the Savesmart, and I'll pay a dollar for every liter-sized square bottle."

"A dollar per bottle? You're kidding."

"Like I said, it's important. Will you tell people?"

"Sure thing, Rev." He took off his right glove to shake my hand. "Thanks."

Next, I called Suzannah.

"What's up?" she asked.

"Hold on. I'll loop Lily in, too."

She accepted the call, and I had two of my best friends on the line. "I need your help tomorrow morning."

"Sure," they both said, simultaneously and without knowing the request. "I have a meeting, but I can move it," Lily added.

Could a girl have better friends?

"Great. Wear work clothes. It could get messy."

Lily emitted a nasal, nervous giggle

"How messy?" Suze asked. Her quick offer of help did not include having stale liquor spilled on her designer jeans.

"As in, clothes you never want to wear again. Meet me at St. Giles' at 9 a.m. tomorrow."

If I told them any more, they might both suddenly have appointments that could not be rescheduled.

"Thanks." I hung up before they could probe or protest.

Kayla texted, *The coast is clear.*

Back at the office, I told her my plan. She designed a flier about my bottle search and ran off photocopies. Then we hung a *Closed* sign on the door of the office and took to the street armed with our staplers and tape gun—what a needlessly violent name for a tool whose danger lay in its serrated blade.

Before 5:00 p.m., we'd distributed all two hundred fliers. Kayla posted hers on telephone poles and streetlights. I passed mine out to the folks who would put them in the hands of the bottle collectors or make a special foray into the world of career recyclers to earn extra cash.

Chapter Twenty-Four

The next morning, the Chronicle's headline read, "Software Engineer Charged in Lesbian Bar-Owner's Murder." In the picture, David wore a goofy look under his shorter, neatly combed hair. I'd have put money on it being the photo from his security badge at the start-up where he worked.

I double-checked my phone. Naomi hadn't called. Hopefully her mom was providing the support she needed.

It didn't come as a surprise when Tish failed to show up to Morning Prayer the next day. Jenny, Lois, Hazel and I enjoyed the service, but I had no time to check in with my new warden afterward—I was a priest-detective on a mission.

Lily and Suze arrived promptly at nine in Suze's BMW and hopped out of the car. Lily wore yoga pants and a fleece, like she was ready for a hike up Mt. Tam. Suze wore jeans, rain boots, and an oversized hoodie from her husband's last concert tour.

"I'll drive."

Suze tossed me the keys. Why she assumed I had a driver's license, I have no idea. Cesar had taught me, but I'd never bothered to take the test.

Lily clicked in a seat belt. "I saw they made an arrest."

"He didn't do it."

"How can you be sure?" Suze asked.

"Let's just say, I've followed the Holy Spirit to this conclusion."

Lily snorted.

I zipped down South Van Ness, then cut over to Mission at Cesar Chavez.

Suze had a death grip on the Oh-shit bar. "Where are we going?"

"Savesmart," I replied, as if I routinely asked them to ditch work and come grocery shopping with me.

"Right. Only I left my reusable bags at home," Lily said.

"I have everything we need." I patted my tote bag on the console between Suze and me. I'd packed a whole box of heavy-duty yard-waste bags along with several hundred dollars in ones. Hopefully that would be enough.

In the back corner of the grocery store's parking lot, a line had formed at the shed where the collectors could redeem their bottles and cans for five-cent deposits. I pulled up to the front of the line in Suze's luxury car. The attendant tried to wave me past. I parked and bolted out of the car. Lily and Suze followed.

An empty plastic milk crate stood against the shed. I nabbed it and turned it upside down, climbing atop where everyone in the line could see me.

"Hi there, folks. I'm looking for a very important whisky bottle. Liter sized. For every one you have, I'll pay you a dollar. Be sure you grab them like this." I borrowed a vodka bottle to demonstrate holding it by the mouth. "We want to preserve any fingerprints."

"You can't do this." A pudgy man in a neon vest waved at me.

"Sure I can."

"I'll call the cops."

"Please do. This search was their job to begin with."

Suze had crossed her arms, and Lily's mouth gaped open. I hopped off the milk crate and handed them each a black garbage bag and an envelope of dollar bills.

"This is about the murder." Suze put her now-full hands on her hips.

Lily slapped her hand over her mouth. "Oh my Gosh, we'll be arrested for interfering in the case."

"Nope. The case is closed. We're not doing anything wrong, but if we get lucky, we might save an innocent man."

The collectors carefully handed us enough bottles to fill four black trash bags. They were too heavy to lift and would never fit in Suze's trunk.

Fortunately, just as the last collector accepted his cash from us, Cesar pulled up in his truck. He gave a wave to the attendant in the shed, then strode our way, frowning so fiercely anyone in their right mind would shake with fear. Anyone but me, of course.

Lily clenched the top of her trash bag. "Uh, oh. A storm just blew in."

Suze leaned down to whisper to me. "Remind me again why you left this guy for girls?"

That wasn't exactly what had happened, and she knew it. But instantly I remembered the feel of Naomi's lips on mine, and my mouth went dry.

"Suzannah, Lily, can I please speak to Alma for a minute alone?"

They both nodded obediently and dove into the car, being sure to roll down the windows for maximum eavesdropping opportunity.

"I said no, so you did it anyway?"

"You said you couldn't spare the officers, so I organized help."

With an index finger, he scratched his eyebrow. "What are the chances it's in there?"

"I can't say. I was never great at math."

"You're perfectly good at math. Whenever you did it without also watching TV and chatting with friends online, you got straight As."

He was right, and I stood a little straighter to know he remembered.

I hefted my bag and moved it toward him an inch. "So, I realize you can't check them all for fingerprints, but I..."

He scowled, and I swallowed the end of my sentence.

"Oh, please, don't stop telling me how you think I should do my job now."

"Well, if blood isn't visible like it was on the shoes, try luminal?"

He nodded. "I was thinking the same thing."

"So, you'll do it?"

He studied my face. "I don't understand you. If you suspect someone else, just tell me who."

The back of my brain itched, my subconscious trying to tell me something. But it wouldn't surface.

"Or is this some cockamamie plan to confess you're the killer? Were you tired of fighting a campaign for justice that was really about bad business when there are kittens to save and homeless people to feed?"

I crossed my arms. Was he serious? He hadn't considered me a suspect from the start, based on our relationship.

"It's David who saves kittens. I focus on the humans."

Cesar rolled his eyes, and I sucked in a deep breath. He was joking.

"I don't know who it was, only that it wasn't David."

"Right." He effortlessly hefted all four bags into the back of his truck and drove off without another word.

A subdued Suzannah drove us out of the lot. At a stoplight, she angled toward me where I sat in the backseat. "So... Cesar?"

I shook my head.

Lily huffed. "It's not fair that you meddled so much in our love lives, and you won't even tell us enough about him to know how we're supposed to meddle."

"He and I are over. Currently, I'm trying to figure out how to get a hot lesbian rabbi who wants to meet a nice Jewish girl to choose me instead."

Suzanna burst into laughter, then caught sight of my face. "Oh, you're serious. Sorry. It's hard to know with you."

Lily giggled. "Thank God for Alma. Without her, our lives would be so boring."

Suze pulled up to St. Giles'. I hopped out of the backseat, then leaned into Lily's window. "Thanks for your help today. Maybe we'll get the rabbi's brother off the hook."

Chapter Twenty-Five

I hated waiting on Cesar to process the bottles. Was he even bothering or just humoring me? But waiting was my only option. I considered buying a lab coat and sneaking into the lab in SOMA for about two seconds before I quit the idea. One thing I could not even pretend at was forensic science—aside from turning wine into it, blood was not on the seminary curriculum. Neither were fingerprints nor luminal.

The police informed Lynn of the arrest and promised to release Cindy's body within 48 hours. I didn't want to discount their promises. From over in Oakland, she video conferenced with me about the funeral, picking music and some readings.

"I'm considering selling the house and moving to L.A.," she said. "It's cheaper to live there, plus I'll be closer to my niece and nephew." Behind her on the screen, her sister bustled around kitchen tidying and cooking.

The muscles in my neck relaxed to know she was well cared for, and her plan seemed wise. "Just give yourself time. You don't have to decide this week."

"Yeah. Good point." She sucked in a breath, nodding and wiping her eyes with a lavender handkerchief. A letter C was embroidered on its corner.

"Call me if you need me."

Her sister appeared over her shoulder. "Thanks for looking after Lynn, Mother Alma."

I hated that particular form of address. To add injury to insult, it now reminded me of tea poisoning. Could Lynn have been the one to send me the toxic courage concoction? She didn't have an alibi to offset her significant motive, and now she was making plans to leave town. Maybe I'd been too quick to accept her grief as genuine.

I should text Cesar about my new suspicion. Except he'd imposed the breakup distance between us again.

I forced a smile for Lynn's sister. "It looks like you're doing a good job caring for her, too."

Lynn turned to hug her, burying her face in her older sibling's shoulder and agreeing with a muffled, "yes."

With the best of intentions not to procrastinate, I tried to work on my sermon. Who had assigned these stupid lessons for the seventh Sunday after Pentecost? Why did Jesus have to resurrect his dead friend Lazarus this week of all weeks? He'd made everything better for Martha and Mary, but I couldn't do a damn thing for Lynn or Naomi.

Kayla appeared in my door. Since witnessing Tish's guerrilla tactics yesterday, she'd stopped shouting questions and requests at me from her desk. The kinder, gentler Kayla asked, "Can you take a call?"

"Sure." Anything to avoid thinking about how Cindy would not be coming back to life and my bishop's committee was staging a *coup d'état.*

I answered the flashing line. "This is Alma."

"Hi, this is Sydney, Al's daughter. He's home, and he'd love a visit when you're free."

"Great. Does now work?"

See what I mean? I preferred to hear his laundry list of my failures than to write a sermon about Lazarus reunited with his happy family.

"Sure. Come on by. You know the address?"

"I do." I'd been to a vestry Christmas party at their flat on Church Street back in December. "I'll be there in twenty minutes."

"Twenty minutes. Great. He's giving me a thumbs-up."

I arrived at their 1920s era building with two flats and rang the bell. Al's daughter came down to open the gate. I followed her up as she filled me in. "They kept him an extra day to make sure his digestive tract was operational, but otherwise he's doing great."

They hadn't warned me in seminary that part of pastoral care involved getting way too much information about people's gastrointestinal health. I'd quickly learned not to ponder what the euphemisms actually meant, for my dignity and that of my parishioners.

"I heard from Jenny Wong that your mom was worried and wanted your dad to resign from his leadership position."

"She's always worried and stressed, no matter what. If Dad leaves the house without her, she resents the reason."

I glanced around.

"Oh, don't worry. She's out to lunch with a friend. I was hoping you could come when she'd gone because she doesn't want him exerting himself or getting wound up. And Dad's upset about her scheming to get him booted off the committee."

"Sydney—is that Reverend Alma?" Al's voice drifted down the hall.

"Yes, Dad, she's right here."

We arrived at the doorway to his bedroom where he sat upright under a neatly tucked bedspread. I'd never seen him out of a coat and tie, but his blue, pinstriped flannel pajamas were far more dignified than a hospital gown.

"You're looking well," I said, which on this occasion wasn't a pastoral nicety.

"Feeling much better, thank you. And thanks also for coming."

Sydney pulled a wooden armchair over to his bedside. "Sit here."

"Thanks." I took the seat, and she slipped from the room. I inhaled a deep breath, then tried to exhale all of my defensiveness. I wasn't a perfect priest by any means. I had flaws, and things to learn. Whatever he had to say, something in his words would help me grow.

"Al, I'm sorry I kept missing you before you went into the hospital." Avoiding him had been a mistake, like running from one angry villager when a whole mob stood at the ready with their pitchforks.

He exhaled. "I know how busy you are, dear. I didn't want to bother you with all your committees, and your visiting, and those long sermon-walks you do, and of course your secret food pantry at the BART Plaza."

I listened for the double edge of criticism in his tone but didn't hear even a hint of it. And had he said...? "You know about that?"

He smiled. "I saw you once on the way home from a baseball game. You had your hood pulled tight, so I could tell it was a private moment for you, and I didn't want to interrupt."

How sensitive of him. "Thanks."

"The bishop called me last week to discuss your work as our priest-in-charge, and if St. Giles' wanted to hire you as our rector. We're three-quarters of the way through your term of appointment, and he reminded me you would need to know whether to begin looking for another job, if we didn't plan to keep you."

"Right." Another job, in another part of the city, or further. Upside: I would never run into Cesar, and I'd never have to cross the threshold where I'd found Cindy's body. Also, it would not be spitting distance from my parents, I wouldn't know my neighbors, it wouldn't be the place where I'd learned I could help the community, that I could make peace.

"Honestly. The time had gotten away from me, Alma. How has a year and a half already passed? Things at St. Giles' have been so busy since you came. So many new people, so much activity. And everything so seamless and natural... People are raving about the pastoral care team Hazel organized, we've embraced a spirit of hospitality under your guidance, and your preaching has been topnotch."

"Um, thanks." My heart raced. Enough with the compliments. If this was that supervision strategy where the bad news came sandwiched in praise, he was giving me a thick slice of bread on top, and I was ready to get to the tofurkey.

"All that is to say, I forgot we had to decide to keep you. I just hoped you'd bless us with your work for a good long time."

Okay. Clearly something was wrong with his brain.

"Al, did anything happen in the hospital? Minor stroke? Did they drop you on your head?" The latter seemed unlikely, but no more so than this entire conversation.

He laughed uncertainly. "What do you mean?"

"I mean, I'd gotten the impression you were less than pleased with my work as priest-in-charge. You're often scowling during coffee hour, and in the bishop's committee meetings, you are bursting with suggestions for what else we can do..."

He looked sheepish. "I'm sorry about the scowling. I'm a bit shy in settings like that. My daughter tells me I have a fierce resting bitch face."

I laughed aloud.

"And I'm sorry if my suggestions seem critical. I don't mean them that way. You've inspired me to dream about what's possible, instead of trying to pinch pennies to keep our doors open longer while our little church dies. We aren't dying anymore. You brought us back to life."

My heart stopped racing and flew up into my throat. Al had just written my sermon about Lazarus. Or more likely, it was the Holy Spirit speaking through him. I glanced up at the ceiling and said a silent, *Thank you*.

"First of all, a priest can't bring a church back to life on her own. We've done it together. And I've seen lots of churches resist a resurrection because they didn't want to change, or welcome different kinds of people, in order to grow."

He beamed like I'd slapped an A+ sticker on his spelling test. "We have, haven't we?"

"But help me out here. During church services, you're writing feverishly on your bulletin, every time I make a mistake in the liturgy, or say something controversial, or a baby cries loudly in the back."

His bushy eyebrows drew together. "I'm not writing those things down. Look in there." He pointed to his bedside table.

Now, my bedside table is full of supplies—the kind made of silicone, and latex, and in purple bottles that read *water-based*—so I hesitated for a moment.

Al might be a curmudgeon, but he wasn't a creep. Hopefully, they kept their supplies on his wife's side of the bed. In fact, hopefully, they had supplies. Even if I didn't like to picture it, for my dignity and that of my parishioners, I always wished for people to enjoy vibrant sex lives well into their old age. For certain, I could trust the evidence of theirs was not waiting for me in the drawer.

I opened it. Inside lay a Bible, bound in burgundy leather with Al's name embossed in gold. And beneath it, a thick stack of bulletins from Sundays at St. Giles'.

"Take them out." He shifted in the bed to watch me and winced.

"Don't move." I drew the bulletins out where he could see me. His handwriting was difficult to decipher. I squinted and crosschecked where he'd made notes with the order of service. Instantly, his words became clear. He'd written little phrases from the prayers and the readings. And, he'd covered the margins with quotes from my sermon.

Oh my. He was listening so closely to the words I dreamed up as I wandered along Valencia and banged my head against my desk on Saturday morning instead of taking a day off.

"I like to meditate on the service before I go to bed."

This wasn't a laundry list of complaints, it was his method of devotion. The head of the bishop's committee thought I was a good priest—except, he wasn't the head anymore. And all this time, Jenny had been warning me that Al disapproved of my work.

"Jenny implied you think I've spread myself too thin. That I don't focus enough on St. Giles."

He blinked. "Not at all. You've trained us to be leaders of our parish so we can do God's work with you, both in the church and out on the streets. That's why we're growing, because you taught us you don't have to be everywhere. It's impressed me from the start, that someone so young could be such an effective delegator."

"But Jenny said—"

His scowl returned, not a resting bitch face, but one active enough to silence me. "I don't know what she's up to. She played right into my wife's anxieties, showing up at the hospital, suggesting I should resign as warden to rest. They decided it all without speaking to me, and she talked the bishop into it."

She hadn't only triangulated us, she'd been misrepresenting his opinions.

"But why?"

His face paled. "I was hoping you'd tell me. I've always found her a delight to work with. Reliable, reasonable, devoted to good causes. And she's always supported you as fervently as I have. Then, on a dime, she changed her tune about you."

Sydney knocked on the doorframe. "Dad, Mom just texted. She's on her way back." She looked at me pointedly.

I stood. "Al, I've got to go. Tons of stuff to do at the office. But you know what—you've totally written my sermon for Sunday, so don't worry about missing it."

He blinked. "All right."

"Also, next time your wife goes out, call the bishop and tell him you want your job back."

He raised his chin. "Right. Good idea."

"Be well." I squeezed his hand. "I'll be back soon."

"No need. I'll be on my feet in no time."

I turned to his daughter. "If that's not true, let me know."

On the way back to St. Giles', I swung by my parents' grocery store. I ordered one of Lee's Gourmet Baskets for the man I hoped would soon be my senior warden again, if I could just figure out what to do about Jenny.

Chapter Twenty-Six

Back at the office, I spent mere seconds in my chair. Thoughts were racing, and I'd never get them organized while staring at these tidy piles on my desk.

I hopped up and over to Kayla. "I need to take a walk and think."

"Right. I'll just tell people you're at that task force on clergy compensation."

"Shit. Is that happening right now?"

"Yeah. In Marin. You'll never make it."

"I could phone in."

"Or, you could go for a walk and contemplate what to do about your bishop's committee trying to depose you. Sometimes you make me crazy, but I'm definitely on team The Devil I Know."

"Aw, that's the nicest thing you've ever said to me."

The sun shone on Valencia Street, warming the sidewalk. It was busy with the after-lunch crowd. Who were these well-dressed young people? Why weren't they behind a desk somewhere pushing pencils? Did they have trust funds or extremely flexible work-from-home setups? How could they afford to linger in coffee shops and stroll along the street all day looking so dapper? Perhaps they were like me, living lean and working hard while I appeared to be hardly working.

The self-named Strange Sam cycled past in the bike lane. He lived in one of the last remaining single room occupancy hotels on Valencia, and he sometimes dropped by the BART Plaza on Sundays for groceries. Marvin Gaye's sweet tenor rang out from his boom box. "Don't punish me with brutality. Talk to me, so you can see, Oh, what's going on, What's going on."

Sam had a penchant for Marvin, and usually I found an extra bounce in my step when he pedaled by, but today the song mocked me. If only I knew what the hell was going on. Who had killed Cindy? And why had Jenny been telling me Al hated me when he was actually my number-one fan?

I kept walking, breathing in the sights and smells of the neighborhood I loved in search of an answer.

I crossed Twenty-second Street. At the curb, a puddle of water had pooled, so black it might have been from a Louisiana swamp. On its surface, rainbow-like ribbons of gasoline swirled, a shimmering blue against the black.

Blue like a shiny sequin on a concrete floor.

Blue like a shimmering evening gown I'd seen on the front page of the Chronicle.

Could the sequin have come off Jenny's dress?

No. She hadn't been at The Carlos Club closing party, she'd been receiving the Friend of Families award. And what motive did she have to kill Cindy? They were friends, allies.

But Jenny was my ally, too, and she was behaving very strangely.

My phone rang. Cesar's name showed on the screen.

"Hello?"

"You're never going to believe this."

"Um. I think I might. You found the bottle with Cindy's blood on it."

"Well, DNA testing takes time, but it matches her type."

"Did you get a fingerprint?"

"Tons, from what appears to be four different people."

"Let me guess… one of them is Supervisor Jenny Wong."

"Damn. How the hell did you know?"

"I think that's her sequin you found on the floor. From the dress she wore to the Friends of Families Awards Banquet. You can see a photo on the cover of last Thursday's Chronicle."

The line went silent, and I tried to guess at his expression. "Please tell me you're thinking, 'Wow, clearly I didn't give Alma enough credit.'"

"Something like that." His voice sounded strained, but without seeing him, I couldn't decipher the emotions in the tone.

"Remember how she came into the office on Thursday and said

she'd heard about Cindy? There wasn't time unless your officers were standing outside St. Giles' announcing the name of the victim to everyone who walked by."

"Damn. How did I miss that?"

And then she'd told him to investigate the hostile reporter, which had been a complete waste of time. Still, those details hardly proved her guilty.

"Isn't this all circumstantial evidence? All we can show for sure is that at some point she touched that bottle."

"Also, if the sequins match, that she was at the bar sometime wearing that dress."

"That's no more evidence than you have against David."

"Right, and she doesn't have a motive I can think of."

"True..." My mind raced to make sense of her behavior. She'd triangulated me and Al, while quite possibly turning the bishop's committee against me.

"I'll bring her in. See if she lies about being at the club, check her alibi."

"Yeah. Good idea."

"Alma."

"Huh?"

"You're getting that far-away sound that tells me you're already off making your own plans."

"I'm not. I'm just thinking."

"Do not. I repeat—do not—approach her about this. If she *is* the killer, she's dangerous."

Jenny Wong, dangerous? What a ridiculous idea. I prayed with her six days a week. But he was right—I'd stay out of it.

My phone buzzed again in my pocket. Probably Cesar calling back to warn me off meddling another time. I pulled it out—Naomi.

Tension eased from my shoulders. She still wanted to be friends.

"Hey, there." I couldn't keep the relief from my voice.

"Hi, Alma." She sounded stiff, stilted, anything but friendly. "I'm having a bit of a problem here. Can you come over?"

"Yeah, sure. Where's here?"

"I'm at David's flat. Something's come up about the case, and I need your help."

Her strange tone didn't match the words, and my stomach

167

twisted. "Listen, I'm sorry about David. But don't give up hope."

"Sure thing. Just come over, okay?" Her voice had gone high, almost piercingly.

Loud swooshing and banging sounds came over the line before the call ended.

Wow. She sounded more upset than I'd expected. Maybe she hadn't leaned on her mom and had been suffering alone.

No. The twist in my gut tightened into a full-on intestinal kink. The edge of panic in Naomi's voice had been too sharp to be simply worry over David. Either this was a side of her I hadn't seen yet, or something was wrong besides David's arrest, something more urgent.

Was she in danger?

I hurried, reaching Abbey Street in eight minutes. Which of the houses had the doorbell camera that had caught David in his socked-feet? I stared at the facades and, spotting two potential cameras, grinned and waved at both for good measure.

Then I rang David Cohen's doorbell. It wasn't Naomi who answered. Out of context, I took a moment to recognize the woman in a black baseball cap, her hair pulled back into a ponytail.

Jenny.

Before I said a word, she grabbed my upper arm and yanked me inside. That was when I saw the gun.

Supervisor Jenny Wong, tireless advocate for the working poor, civil liberties, and affordable housing. In case you don't live in San Francisco or happen to know anyone of Jenny's—and my—political persuasion, we don't like guns. They keep us about as safe as Nazis do.

And yet, here was the self-appointed head of my bishop's committee pointing a handgun at me.

Okay, Cesar, here's where I admit to being a Pollyanna. Staring down the barrel of her gun, I could hardly believe she was pointing it at me.

Despite my shock, I still managed a very priestly response. "What the hell, Jenny?"

She waved the gun, indicating I should walk upstairs. Thank God Aviva's stuffed bear wasn't in the doorway to witness this coercion.

"Do you even know how to use that thing?"

"It's actually quite self-explanatory." She laughed, shrill and maniacal.

Uh oh. This was not good.

Naomi whimpered. She sat on the couch in the living area at the top of the stairs, whole and unharmed, but parchment pale.

"What's going on?" I asked her.

Jenny answered. "You've made a mess. Such a big fucking mess. And now I need your help to fix it."

It seemed like the wrong time to point out that the person who made the mess was the one who'd killed Cindy, not me.

"Give me your phone." Jenny held out her hand, not wavering with her gun. And if she did waver, what would I do, tackle her? Yeah, right.

She dropped the device into her pocket. Crap. So much for pressing record and secretly capturing a confessional monolog. Once again, life failed to live up to mom's cop shows.

"Sit down." Again, Jenny pointed with the weapon. "We have a lot of work to do."

I took a seat next to Naomi.

"I'm so sorry," she whispered. "When she told me to call you, she wasn't like this, hadn't shown me the gun, or I never would have agreed. She told me she's a member of your church and she wanted to tell us something about the case."

I exhaled. Nice to know Naomi hadn't opted to sacrifice me for her own safety. "I don't understand," I whispered back. "How did she even know we're friends?"

"I visited Kearney Properties again to ask about the keys."

Damn. Naomi shouldn't have done that, especially not alone. But I couldn't blame her. The keys were still a loose end, and she was desperate to exonerate her brother.

"She was there. She came downstairs, told me she knows you, offered me a ride home…"

"I happened to be visiting Kevin at the time to discuss the affordable housing project in China Basin. He recognized Naomi as your friend despite her sunhat and reflective glasses." She flicked her gaze to Naomi. "Apparently he remembered your mouth, which he had some rather crude things to say about, the pig."

It made sense. Her lips were memorable even before you'd tasted them, felt them on your ear and the hollow of your neck.

"Did he give you the keys to The Carlos Club that night?"

She shook her head. "The night desk person is my second cousin."

"Eventually, the police will figure that out, Jenny."

"I don't think so." She was shaking her head.

"They already have quite a lot of circumstantial evidence against you."

"That won't hold up." She paced, the gun hanging loose at her side. "I could have been in the bar any night, left my prints there anytime... Just like all of Cindy's friends."

It would have been an excellent moment to attack her if I wasn't five feet tall and with zero martial arts skills. If I got out of this one alive, I would need to up my self-defense game. Kung Fu? Jiu Jitsu? Or something more badass, like Krav Maga?

"That's why I need your help." She stopped pacing and leveled her gaze right at me. "We can't have David Cohen take the blame. But we are three smart women, and you have Detective Garza's ear. Surely we can think of some way to cover this up."

"Why on earth would I do that? You killed my friend."

She brandished the gun at me. "For the good of the neighborhood, the city. San Francisco needs me."

An involuntary gurgle of disgust came out of my mouth, and Jenny scowled.

Naomi elbowed me in the ribs. "Yes, it does need you, Supervisor. How can we help?"

Okay. The rabbi had a point. It was generally a good policy to agree with the person pointing a gun at you.

Jenny smiled her campaign smile at Naomi. "I've given this a lot of thought, and it seems to me we need to plant misleading evidence."

"You mean frame someone else?" Again, I couldn't keep the disgust from my voice.

"Not someone specific. We just need to direct the detective away from David, to confuse the investigation so that they aren't able to close the case, and eventually it will go cold."

"And Cindy will have no justice, and you'll get away with murder?"

"Justice? Justice is affordable housing for working families. Justice is making sure everyone in the city has access to health care. Justice is *not* keeping a stinking, poorly run bar open to feed Cindy's ego."

Her ego? My spine went rigid.

As if Naomi sensed my tension, she brown nosed our captor a little more. "Your work is so important. Alma and I want to help make sure you are able to continue it. Did you have any ideas about how to mislead the police?"

Jenny huffed. "Sadly, I'm all out of ideas. But little miss can't mind her own business is full of ideas." She waved her gun at me rather haphazardly, and I gulped. How likely was it to fire accidentally?

"I tried to warn you off," she said. "That tea was supposed to make you sick for days, and I needed you laid up, distracted for a while. If you kept poking around in the case—"

"I would have realized that you arrived at church Thursday morning already knowing Cindy's fate, and you threw out the lead about the reporter to send Cesar in the wrong direction."

"Exactly."

Her tea had worked if you considered how long it took me to realize she'd incriminated herself mere moments after I'd found the body.

"And then you made me think I was losing support at church so I would refocus there."

"And that didn't work either. You refused to stay out of it and made my life a living hell. So now, you think of something, Alma."

Her life had been hell? What about Lynn? What about David and Naomi? What about me, unable to look at the stoop of my church without remembering my friend's dead body?

"I already thought of it. How about you take responsibility for your actions and confess to God and the police?"

"Oh, shut up. This is serious." Her gun arm shook and the weapon itself made a frightening clicking sound.

Naomi whispered. "This isn't the best time to get self-righteous."

Chapter Twenty-Seven

Naomi was right. Jenny appeared to be hanging onto her sanity by a strand of dental floss, along with this delusion that she could cover up her sins and continue as if nothing had changed.

I tried for a gentler tone. "I still don't understand what happened that night. Why don't you tell me, and maybe I'll think of some way to help you."

"Yes. Yes. Good idea. While you attended the party, I was sitting next to Scots Richard at the awards dinner."

I nodded. The gay activist and philanthropist had been a major donor to Jenny's first campaign.

She continued. "Cindy texted him, pleading for money to help her keep The Carlos Club open. I've been waiting for a second donation from him, but it's been slow to come. At the event, I tried to talk him out of getting involved with Cindy, reminded him of the importance of staying focused on affordable housing, but he wouldn't listen."

Now probably wasn't the time to remind Jenny that Cindy's eviction and the rise of rent were both the direct result of gentrification. Their causes were overlapping and inseparable.

"He told her he'd send her fifty-thousand dollars." Her voice hitched. "I need that money for my campaign, or I'll never beat Alvarez. So I went to the Carlos Club to convince Cindy to turn down Richard's money and give up her fight. She'd hijacked everyone's goodwill with her stupid cause. Saving a bar, for God's sake. Meanwhile, important issues were going unnoticed because she stole the attention with her purple hair and her personal attacks on Kevin Kearney, like the whole thing was a reality TV show.

That's not how change happens."

"Let me guess. When you got to the bar, she wouldn't listen?"

"Exactly," Jenny said. "She insisted it was a matter of principle. And then… she threatened me."

"Aha!" Naomi interjected. "There's your solution. You can plead self-defense."

But no. The final detail fell into line, and I finally understood the note on the napkin in Cindy's office, when she'd drawn her plan for a human chain. *J/K!* didn't mean just kidding.

"Jenny doesn't mean Cindy threatened her physically."

"Oh." Naomi slumped back into the sofa as Jenny nodded in confirmation.

"She figured out you'd made some kind of deal with Kevin Kearny, and she threatened to expose you."

"Yes." Jenny sniffed, a wave of grief seeming to rise up in her from nowhere. "In exchange for ten affordable units in his next development, all the supervisors on the Land Use Committee vetoed listing The Carlos Club as a historic landmark. I don't know how she found out, but she called me a hypocrite, and said I'd sold her out for ten measly apartments. Measly! That's ten families who will have safe, clean homes."

Personally, I agreed with Jenny. But was the criticism enough of a reason for her to grab a whiskey bottle and smash it onto Cindy's head?

"I don't understand. You killed her for calling you a hypocrite? It's not like you to lose your temper."

"No, it's not." With her gunless hand, she smoothed her hair. "But one story accusing me of backroom deals could tip the election in Alvarez's favor. I have to be better than that. I've spent my whole life championing the downtrodden, and I could not let her ruin my image."

Her image. I shuddered. We all failed to live up to our standards of goodness sometimes or were forced to compromise our ideals. We had to face up to these truths, accept reality, and do our best. But instead, Jenny had killed Cindy to protect her ugly secret—that she was as human as every other politician in the world.

"God knows what you did, Jenny, and God still loves you."

"Oh, screw that, Alma. I have come way too far to crumple and make a tearful confession." She cocked the gun. "Now, are you going to help me, or are you going to make this hard?"

Dammit. I'd begun to shake.

Next to me on the couch, Naomi squeezed my fingers. I glanced at her, needing an anchor. Her eyes were wide and unblinking. She sat still, tightly coiled and alert. I sensed energy but not fear buzzing just beneath her surface.

"Okay. Okay. Let me think. I can tell Cesar that I just now remembered seeing a pack of ethnically non-distinct youth fleeing the scene. How's that?"

Jenny sighed. "Alma, you are not leaving me with many choices." She shook the gun. Her voice had turned brittle and cold.

"It's okay," Naomi said, breathy and panicked. "We'll think of something, right Alma?"

"No. It's too late." Jenny's shoulders sagged, and the corners of her mouth pulled downward. "I see now that if I let you go, you'll run straight to the police. I didn't want to hurt David the other night, and I don't want to hurt you, believe me. But I can't go to prison." She laughed, loud and shrill. Someone less feminist than me might have called the sound hysterical.

Fear screamed in my head, made it impossible to think. There wasn't even room in my brain to gloat that I'd been right about the attempted hit-and-run, and Cesar had been wrong.

Jenny gestured with her weapon. "Stand up. I didn't want it to come to this, but we are going for a drive in David's car to find a nice place for a fiery accident."

The now familiar lump in my throat swelled so huge I couldn't swallow a breath. My mentor and friend had resorted to murder to protect her image and the career it fueled. Now she was threatening Naomi and me. Cesar was right—evil could lurk in anyone. If I didn't think of something, it might be the end of us.

"Get up." She waved the gun. "Down the back stairs and into the garage."

Damn. If only David took public transportation like me. Jenny could hardly hijack an Uber.

We stood. Jenny tossed Naomi the keys. "You drive. Alma, lead the way, single file through the kitchen and no funny business or I shoot your friend."

Had she read my mind? I'd imagined grabbing a knife from the block. The one I'd used to cut carrots for stir-fry was nice and sharp.

Jenny stuck the barrel of the gun into Naomi's back, and she yelped.

Shit. Think of something! But what? I moved through the dark hallway, searching the kitchen ahead for an idea. With Naomi between us, I could hardly open a cabinet door and slam it into Jenny's face.

I stepped into the kitchen. The fire extinguisher hung on the wall near the back door. Could I grab it and shoot flame retardant before Jenny realized what was happening?

"Hey," Jenny cried.

Behind me, a crack sounded. I spun and found Jenny flat on the ground, her forehead bleeding. Next to her, a dining chair lay on its side.

Naomi lunged for the gun, but Jenny lifted it toward her. In a blur of movement, Naomi kicked the weapon from Jenny's hand.

I scrambled to catch it while Naomi dove for Jenny, as agile as Bruce Lee reincarnated. Holy cow. Apparently Naomi did know Kung Fu.

"Quick. Phone." She pointed to the landline.

Gun in one trembling hand, I dialed 911 left handed. Jenny had begun screaming and cursing as I tried to explain the situation to the emergency dispatcher. I think she scarcely believed me, but I stayed on the line, and soon I heard the sirens coming.

I kept the gun trained on Jenny, but Naomi had completely subdued her, sitting astride her prone form, my warden's wrists held in a firm grip. Naomi's cheeks were flushed like they'd been when we'd fooled around, and her breasts heaved. My mouth went dry.

Damn. What kind of pacifist got turned on watching the object of her desire kick lady-ass?

"Where the hell did you learn that?" I asked.

"I lived in Israel for a year in college and took martial arts classes with this ex-Mossad guy. It's great exercise."

Israeli self-defense? "As in Krav Maga?" All her whimpers and yelps had fooled me, and Jenny too, it seemed.

"You've heard of it?"

"Yeah. And as soon as we hand her over to Cesar, I'm signing up for lessons." Somehow it rankled that she'd been the one to save me, just as she'd first deduced my profession.

Not that I'm competitive, I just prefer to be the one surprising people.

The police entered with stealthy moves, then shouts.

"Drop the weapon. Drop it!" A man in black Kevlar shouted. He seemed to be looking right at…

Oh, right. Me. I was holding a gun. I set it down gingerly and kicked it away from myself the way I'd seen it done on Mama's cop shows. Man, she would have hated to miss all the action.

I explained who I was, and Naomi, and Jenny. My warden, the supervisor of District Nine, tried to shout over my words as I spoke, which only made her look more nuts.

When they cuffed Jenny's hands, Naomi climbed off her. She flew into my arms, soft and warm and a lot stronger than she looked. Her embrace stilled my shakes.

"I am so sorry. I should've known better than to call you. I should have handled it myself."

"No. Don't say—"

She took hold of my head with both hands and silenced me with a kiss, hard and deep enough to make my toes curl and forget we had an audience of six patrol officers.

Someone entered on heavy feet, announcing his presence with a noisy clearing of the throat. There's only one cough in the world I would recognize. Cesar's.

I pulled back.

"So you closed the case for me?" Cesar asked.

I didn't reply. If it weren't for Naomi being a secret badass, I might have ended my short stint as an amateur detective at the bottom of a cliff somewhere.

Rolling his eyes, he said, "Of course you did." To his credit, he sounded equally amused and irritated.

"It wasn't just me. Naomi brought her down." I squeezed her hand.

"I was scared to death. That woman is not in her right mind." She sighed breathily, not sounding for a second like a Krav Maga master.

At David's kitchen table, we told Cesar everything that Jenny had confessed to us. Naomi didn't leave my side, even after the police left. They released David in the late afternoon, and Christina came over and coddled all three of us. She remembered my dietary preferences and made a garlicky vegan pasta dish with white beans and kale that even satisfied the meat eaters. David opened wine he'd been saving for a special occasion, like being cleared of murder charges.

We sank into the deep, old couch in the living room, Naomi's head on my shoulder. Christina and David occupied a single, wide armchair.

Suddenly, Naomi sat up straight. "Now, I have to ask, genius brother of mine, what the hell were you thinking, dumping your shoes and walking home in your socks?" Her tone was a tad harsh.

He shielded his eyes with his hand.

I sat up too, ready to defend him.

David sighed. "When I found her dead, I was in shock. I'd gone back there so full of righteous anger, and I knew I'd look guilty. Hell, I felt a little guilty, like I was looking at what I might have done, if I'd let all my bottled-up stress out, Mr. Hyde style—"

Naomi dismissed his words with a wave of her hand. "You couldn't do something like that—"

"Couldn't anyone, if they were desperate enough?" He poured himself more wine.

Jenny's actions had me wondering the same thing. In answer to her brother's question, Naomi took a gulp of wine.

"I'd like to think I'm better than Supervisor Wong," he added. "That something was broken in her, but I guess it doesn't take much to break a person like that."

Christina patted his thigh and snuggled closer to him. He turned the T.V. on, setting the volume low. A beautiful nature documentary played. "I show this to calm Aviva down sometimes. At least I used to… "

The misery in his words brought stinging tears to my eyes. But he was right about the video. The images took my mind off to exotic places far less menacing than my neighborhood had become. Even with a full belly and the pleasant fog of alcohol, it took hours for the adrenaline to bleed out of me completely. From the way Naomi kept hold of me, our fingers interlocked, I knew she felt the same way.

My eyelids grew heavy. I turned my head to Naomi and whispered against her shiny hair. "Time for me to head home."

"No, don't go. I want you to stay." She squeezed my hand, hot in hers.

Every reason I'd stopped things on my couch two days earlier remained. But they seemed distant and blurry compared to her warm brown eyes and the hint of red on her gorgeous lips.

I could go home to my little house, behind the place where I'd found Cindy's body, the place where I'd prayed every morning with the woman who'd murdered her, then planned to kill me to cover it up. Or I could stay with Naomi so we could comfort each other.

It would have been an easy choice with anyone I wanted less—a bit of fun and feeling good to ward off the cold deep inside me. But with her, so easy to be with, so easy to imagine getting close to, falling for… It felt reckless.

I am many things—spontaneous and impulsive included—but I am not reckless.

I closed my eyes and offered up a prayer. *What now?*

The answer came in the tingles that filled me when she kissed my cheek, the jolt of electricity that shot up my arm when she tugged me to standing.

I followed her into the bedroom, and we didn't talk at all about what would come next.

Chapter Twenty-Eight

Dawn crept around the shades in David's spare bedroom. Naomi breathed steadily, asleep at my side in a twin bed.

Gently, I extricated myself from her arms, dressed silently, and tiptoed out of the flat.

A stinking, steaming pile of mess awaited me at St. Giles', thanks to Jenny Wong. I was not looking forward to the explanations and sermons I would have to give, making theological sense of the fact that one of our wardens had let something evil take hold of her good purposes.

I slid into my house, showered, and made tea just in time for Morning Prayer.

As I reached the front steps, where a shrine to Cindy had sprung up overnight, Lois, Hazel, and a gray-faced Al arrived. He leaned on a cane for support. Sad eyes and thin mouths informed me they'd heard the news. It was probably in the paper.

I ran my fingers through my damp hair. "Would you mind if we meditated in silence this morning?"

"Sounds perfect, dear." Lois squeezed my arm.

Tish, our other regular, did not appear. Perhaps she'd realized she'd fallen sway to Jenny's schemes. I ought to call her soon to assure her I had no hard feelings about her investigation into church finances.

Kayla had opened the office and turned on the lights earlier than her usual start time. The Chronicle lay on her desk. The headline read *High Priestess of Mission Street Breaks Murder Wide Open*.

Oh great. Just what I needed.

It featured archived photos—me, arms raised in victory, at a rally outside the medical marijuana clinic, and one I recognized from Jenny's website—her in a navy suit, the U.S. and California flags draping from poles behind her.

Kayla stepped out of my office. "Hey. The phone's been ringing off the hook. I left you a stack of new messages."

"Great." I couldn't keep the weariness from my voice.

She winced, her mouth arching into a sympathetic frown. "You okay?"

I shrugged. "I guess."

The door opened. A man with salt-and-pepper hair and a purple shirt stepped in.

A layer of sweat formed on my palms. "Bishop Vasquez."

"Hello, Alma. Since you refuse to return my phone calls, I decided to drop by."

Fair enough. "Sorry. The murder sort of took over my life. It's all I could think about or focus on."

"Trauma is like that. I would have liked to offer my pastoral support to you. But I supposed you had things perfectly under control."

Kayla snorted.

I glared at her, then extended my arm to indicate the door. "Please, come into my office."

He settled himself in the chair across from my desk—an odd feeling to be facing the man I'd vowed to obey while I occupied the position of authority in the room. "How are you holding up?"

I exhaled. "I'm okay. A little shaken."

He nodded, encouraging me to continue. He had a pockmarked face with deep creases along his mouth, and it could have looked sinister. But he clasped his hands over his purple paunch and smiled sweetly, the picture of pastoral listening.

Where did I start? "Bishop, I'm not sure what the paper says, but Jenny Wong… "

"Yes, yes. Captain Tang apprised me of the whole situation last night. What a shock. I'd spoken to her just the other day about your bishop's committee."

"Yes. That was part of her ploy to discredit me because she'd incriminated herself, although I hadn't realized it. She pretended to support me while she took Al's place as head of the committee and staged a coup."

"I see." He cleared his throat. "We could have avoided that if you'd only returned my calls last week."

"I know. But I didn't understand her behavior at the time. She was very skillful in her manipulations, convincing me she was my ally. Meanwhile the police needed my help, and the victim's family, and—"

"And you yourself were in shock about finding your friend dead."

"Yes." I didn't add that my impulse to let the spirit guide me kept leading me back to the case.

"Captain Tang says you were a great help. Your knowledge of the neighborhood, your—"

"Nosiness?"

Bishop Vasquez chuckled. "I believed he called it tenacity, and he also mentioned you work well with his top detective, Garza."

"Yes. We're old friends."

A sparkle in the man's eye hinted Captain Tang might have suggested Cesar and I were a bit more than just old friends. Well, not anymore.

"He threatened to give you a scholarship to the police academy."

A laugh burst from me. "Not to worry, Bishop. You're stuck with me."

"Good, good. As long as we can we agree that in the future, you will return my phone calls promptly?" His tone was gentle, but it did not allow me to forget I had vowed to obey him at my ordination.

"Yes, sir."

"I have a question about the case. Captain Tang said you found the murder weapon at the recycling center. How did it get there?"

Wanting to appear humble to my bishop, I suppressed the urge to say, *Elementary, Vasquez,* and cut straight to the point.

"Apparently, Jenny dumped it in a blue bin on her walk home from the murder and considered it disposed of. She forgot about the collectors who make their living redeeming the bottles and cans for pennies. One of them picked up the bottle along with the hundreds of others and brought it to the Savesmart recycling center. Kayla and I put out word I'd pay a dollar per bottle, then Lily and Suzannah went with me to gather them. They're very good friends."

He chuckled. "As are you for giving them credit. Now, why is the paper calling you the high priestess of Mission Street?"

I groaned and rested my forehead in my hands. "It's just a joke. It started when I worked to help a medical marijuana clinic keep its lease. But I promise I never touch the stuff. I'll take a drug test, if you'd like."

He wagged his finger. "No need for that. Marijuana is legal now. It does wonders for my mothers' arthritis."

"Um… That's great. I'm glad to hear it."

"Nonetheless, I'd rather not see your nickname on the front page of the Chronicle again. Not the image we're going for as a church." He scratched his chin.

"I'm not planning to make the front page again soon, Bishop."

"Still… I'll call Connie Hall and ask her to exercise a little more editorial restraint."

Wow. Bishop Vasquez was well connected—the Editor and Chief of the Chronicle, Captain Tang. Was he buddies with the mayor and Dianne Feinstein too? Had he admired Jenny Wong as much as I did?

"Speaking of pastoral care, I have to admit, I'm reeling. A person I trusted, who I prayed with almost every day, who stood up for the poor, the oppressed—she killed my friend and planned to kill me."

He inhaled deeply and nodded. "I wish I had an easy answer for you. It's one of the hardest things I've faced in ministry—how good people can abuse trust and hide terrible secrets. Our job is to keep proclaiming God's love and help bring healing. I trust you can do it. In fact, Alma, I couldn't be more pleased with your work at St. Giles'."

"Thank you, sir."

"And from what I hear, your parishioners love you. Call my secretary, and let's set up a meeting with your committee so they can offer you a letter of agreement to be their rector."

Mrs. Cohen flew in from New Jersey that afternoon. Naomi and David took her to dinner. They definitely needed family time, and I didn't mind not being invited.

Naomi came to my place straight from the restaurant. At the door, she kissed my cheek, a hint of sweet red wine on her breath.

She dropped onto my couch and rested her feet on the coffee table. "So, my mom loves Christina."

"Wow." I hadn't expected that.

"I know. I think she understood how unhappy David and Melissa were together better than I had. She saw how much Christina adores him, and every mother of a son wants her little boy to be some woman's prince."

It was a sweeping statement, but Mrs. Garza, for one, had felt the same way.

Then her words sank in. Christina has been invited to dinner, and I hadn't. Well, obviously they were far more serious than me and Naomi. If we were anything, we were just getting started. Maybe Mrs. Cohen accepting one gentile into the family boded well for our prospects.

Naomi leaned forward to kiss me, unbuttoning my clerical shirt and sliding one hand inside my bra. All thoughts of her mother flew from my mind, and I let her lower me onto the couch.

Lynn scheduled Cindy's funeral for Wednesday. She wanted to keep it small. Every patron or customer of The Carlos Club did not need to be a part of her grief.

A group of close family and friends attended the service, along with a few of the old timers at St. Giles'. The Morning Prayer crowd who'd prayed alongside Jenny Wong for years were struggling to make sense of her actions. Their good friend and rising political star had been the one who brought death to their doorstep.

Like the bishop, I had no easy answers for them—ambition, anger, the powerful instinct to preserve her life at any cost. Those things had led Jenny to evil, and I pitied her for it.

A few parishioners lowered their voices and whispered, "How can I trust anyone?"

"Do not let Jenny's actions steal your faith in others," I insisted over and over again. "That is letting her sin continue to harm us."

People like Lois and Tish seemed to take my words to heart although they grieved for the friend they'd known and trusted. If I was hired as rector of St. Giles', we'd have a lot of work to do to heal from Jenny's betrayals.

For a week, Naomi slept at my place, so her mom could have David's spare bed. If Mrs. Cohen inquired where she was spending her nights, Naomi didn't mention the conversation. I avoided asking if they'd discussed me for fear of hearing nothing had changed, and these sweet, contented days were just a blip soon to be over.

Mrs. Cohen left, satisfied that her children were safe, settled, and that Christina would take care of David. Naomi went back to officially sleeping at her brother's, but she stayed at my place every other night. On those evenings, I cooked, she cleaned, and we scoured apartment listings to help her find a place. She relied on my knowledge of the city to hone her search. Neither of us brought up the Cohen family rule, which had bent for Christina and David.

The night she signed a lease, she brought takeout to my house, setting a reusable tote filled with a tower of cardboard boxes on my coffee table.

"It's time we talked."

Her tone told me all I needed to know. I flung myself back on the couch and barely resisted crossing my arms. "If that's the way it is, there's nothing to talk about."

She frowned, lip trembling. "That's the way it is."

"What about Christina?"

"Mom is making peace with her because she wants David to be happy. But the Cohen family rule is important to me, too. If I give up now, I'll never know if that woman is out there, wanting the life I've always wanted."

"You know I would never ask you to give up your traditions, your faith."

"I know. But you have your own, and I respect them. I want to raise a big family like the one I grew up with, not one trying to practice two religions."

Mutt that I am, I could rail against her ideal of homogeneity, but it wasn't about sameness for her. It was about being thoroughly immersed in her culture so she could preserve it. I found it impossible not to respect that longing.

Plus, there was the whole wanting a big family hitch. The motherhood gene had skipped me, or maybe I just poured out all my maternal instincts on the people of St. Giles' and our neighborhood.

Turns out, I wasn't a big enough person to admit that I also failed to meet her requirements in this way, so I kept my mouth shut on the subject. She was perfect for me, but I was not right for her—an all-too-familiar feeling.

The lump swelled in my throat.

"I understand." I scooted to the edge of the cushion and unpacked the food from her bag. "Thanks for dinner. I'll get plates and forks."

When I returned with them, she hadn't taken a seat.

I bent and re-stacked the boxes in her bag.

She waved her arms in protest. "Keep the food."

"I've lost my appetite." It sounded a smidge passive aggressive, I know, but truly, I couldn't imagine getting food past the emotion goiter in my throat. I would uncork a bottle of something and drink a liquid dinner.

She left, and the sudden, stark emptiness of house pressed in on me. I'd had breakups before, if you could even call this ending by the term. Only one had ever hurt so badly—the time Caesar left, walking away from our good thing because I couldn't be what he wanted.

I'd only known Naomi a few weeks, but this pain felt years in the making.

Chapter Twenty-Nine

Three weeks later, I was walking back to the office from a task force meeting at the hospital when a truck barreled down the street and pulled up onto the sidewalk in front of St. Giles', stopping mere feet from me. A stream of expletives queued up in my mouth before I recognize the man behind the steering wheel.

He hopped out, wearing jeans and a sweater. "Get in."

My heart leapt into my throat. Did he want my help on a case again? Solving another murder would be a perfect distraction from Naomi's absence, especially if I didn't know the victim and the culprit personally.

"What happened?" The excitement lifted the pitch of my voice.

He blinked. "Nothing. I just need to talk to you."

"Oh." Something inside me resisted, pressing my sternum back and away from him. Was that my friend the Holy Spirit warning me off? "It's the middle of the workday. I have tons to do in the office."

"Since when does that matter? You're never in your office."

He had a point. I complied, texting Kayla that I was meeting with Detective Garza and wasn't sure when I'd return. Then I climbed into the passenger seat.

He rounded the block and headed west. "Where are we going?"

"Beach."

Tingles cascaded over my scalp. The beach was our spot. Particularly an isolated little cove north of Fort Funston. You could only reach it at low tide, and only then if you scrambled down a cliff and up again before the tide came in.

I hadn't been there since we split up, partly because it was our special place, partly because I'd only descend that slope if Cesar were at the bottom to catch me. Although, come to think of it, I'd trust Naomi, the Krav Maga master, too.

"Why the beach?" I asked.

"Like I said, I need to talk to you."

We'd always done our best talking there, but there was nothing more to say. We made the trip in silence. In the parking lot, we left our shoes in his truck. The sight of his bare feet seemed strange, intimate, like seeing him naked again. We trekked north, past the well-worn paths where dog-owners let their pets run off leash.

The trail to our cove seemed narrower than I remembered. The cliff had eroded since the last time we'd come, making the drop even more steep and treacherous.

If we climbed down, how the hell would we get back up? Even in July, the water was too damn cold, the waves too strong to swim.

He must have sensed my reservation.

"Come on." His gaze held answers to all the arguments I might make. We didn't need to speak them.

I crammed my toes in the footholds until, halfway, the trail turned into a ramp of loose soil. I slid down fast onto the wet, compact sand at the bottom.

He spread out a towel, and we sat, watching the surf roar ten feet beyond our toes. After several long minutes, I felt him shift toward me.

"I missed you."

"It's only been few weeks."

"I missed you for a whole year before that. Every damn day. And I'm so goddamn sorry."

He didn't owe me an apology. It had been abrupt, felt harsh at the time, the way he'd slammed the door on our history together. But soon I'd seen it was necessary—going cold tofurkey was the only way for us to make a break. All our patterns and habits would have sucked us back together as they had so many times before.

"I missed you, too. But I understood, and you were right."

"No, I wasn't right. Seeing you again, your help with the case, it showed me I was dead wrong."

"Cesar, you know yourself and what you want. I'm not it. Seeing each other stirred stuff up again, but it will settle down. Let's be friends."

187

"No. I made a mistake. We need to try again."

I breathed in his words. They tingled through me, but they didn't settle in my stomach.

"Was I right about the girl?"

I blew out the breath. "I don't think she was using me to get to you. We were great together, but she wants a nice Jewish girl to settle down with. So yeah, I guess you were."

He flung himself back on the sand, his laughter echoing off the cliff behind us.

I punched his upper arm. "What?"

He couldn't stop laughing long enough to answer.

My throat tensed. "Knock it off."

"I'm sorry." He was still laughing and clearly not at all sorry.

"What is so funny?"

"Alma, you have to see. You're always trying to be everything to everyone, but one thing you can't be is Jewish. It's an object lesson in accepting your limitations."

I laid next to him on my side, pouting. "I don't like limitations."

His laughing gentled, and his eyes softened. "I know, baby. I know."

The words melted some place inside me, and I needed to protect the soft mushy spot fast.

"Cesar, it's the same between us. You want something from me that I can't be."

He shook his head. "I did. But since Cindy's murder, I realized no one can compare to you. I've revised my ideal. Now it's you."

"Oh."

Worst possible time to have this conversation. I was still hurting from Naomi's rejection, and his words were such a sweet salve. With our history, it would be so easy to tilt my face toward him, to let him kiss me. He would know I wasn't making any promises, wouldn't he?

He moved toward me, his broad shoulders so strong and comforting. I held up my palm and pressed it against his chest.

"Don't say no." He covered my hand. "Promise you'll think about giving us another try."

"Okay. I'll think about it."

The next day, David Cohen left an invitation with Kayla when I was out of the office. Upon returning, I opened the envelope.

Naomi's Place, Grand Opening, Friday 8:00 p.m. He'd written, *Would love to see you. We're so grateful, please come to the opening night.*

Beneath his message was a single word in a different handwriting. *Please! -N.*

I didn't want to go.

The renovation had moved fast, but I'd peered in through the window several times and it looked a thousand times better than The Carlos Club.

Words showed through the paper, printed on the reverse side of the invitation. I flipped it over and discovered a cocktail menu. The first drink listed was called The Cindy. *Zaya rum, Mexican Coke, Meyer lemon bitters, lime peel garnish. Served on the rocks.*

I hadn't felt the lump in my throat for weeks, but now it returned, swelling with sadness and bittersweet love for my friend.

"Are you going to go?" Kayla appeared at my side, reading the invitation.

"Maybe." I wanted to see Naomi, and she wanted to see me. But I'd spent the night lying awake, thinking about Cesar's request that I give us another try. If I had to face her again, I might need him at my side to help me resist her pull.

The phone rang.

Kayla answered. "St. Giles'."

She frowned. "Yes, she's right here." She passed me the phone. "It's the bishop."

Uh oh. What had I done now? "Hello, Bishop."

"Alma, thank God." He blew out a breath. "I need your help. There's been a murder at the cathedral."

THE END

If you enjoyed reading *All Things*, you may also like these
titles by Amber Belldene

The Hot Under Her Collar Series
contemporary romance
Not A Mistake
Not Over Yet
Not Another Rock Star

The Siren Series
paranormal romance
The Siren's Touch
The Siren's Dance
The Siren's Dream

Blood Vine
paranormal romance
Blood Vine
Blood Entangled
Blood Reunited